You Otter Be in Pictures

by

Kate Berberich

Surf, Sand and Romance

You Otter Be in Pictures

Cover Art by *Tina Lynn Stout*

The Wild Rose Press, Inc.
PO Box 708
Adams Basin, NY 14410-0708
Visit us at www.thewildrosepress.com

Publishing History
First Edition, 2025
Trade Paperback ISBN 978-1-5092-6162-8
Digital ISBN 978-1-5092-6163-5

Surf, Sand and Romance
Published in the United States of America

Dedication

With gratitude to the staff of the Kenmore Branch
Library for tables to edit on, rooms to speak in, and
unceasing patience with all my weird research requests.

Chapter One

Sophie Bennet spit out the single strand of red hair which had escaped from her braid and continued her tour. "So, the recovery of Regency Bay has been dependent on community-wide efforts in recycling and—dude, seriously?" The last was addressed to the member of her tour group who'd just dropped an empty plastic water bottle on the boardwalk—three feet from an array of recycling bins and a large "Thank You for Not Littering" sign—and kept right on walking.

Old Frank paused his sweeping the boardwalk in front of Seaside Sundries' neat white shingles and aqua door, to glare at the offender over the steel rims of his glasses. The kid pushing the cart from Napoleon's Nuts looked utterly appalled. And Deputy Bonnie appeared from around a corner, pulling her ticket book and pen from a pocket of her uniform cargo shorts.

A fellow who'd been trailing along at the end of the group taking pictures with a few grand worth of camera equipment stooped and picked up the bottle, read the labels on the bins, and dropped it in the correct one. He had luscious black hair a bit overdue for a trim, a couple days' worth of scruff, and the most amazing green eyes.

Down, girl. "Thank you, sir. And you"—she pointed at the litter bug—"this is your one and only warning. Littering is prohibited, and your next offense will have you removed from the boardwalk. You can pay your ticket at the office on the corner." She nodded toward town hall, situated at the corner where the boardwalk intersected Austen Boulevard.

"Ticket? For what? You can't—"

"Actually, she can," Deputy Bonnie informed him sweetly. "She's the mayor." She handed him the citation. "Have a nice day."

Sophie sucked in a deep breath of salt air and continued her spiel. "Securing the funds for our recycling center and water treatment plant meant the whole town making a commitment to green living. You'll notice any beverages you purchase on the boardwalk are served in paper cups with paper straws. Can anyone tell me why?"

A pigtailed little girl wearing glittery purple framed glasses bounced up and down on the toes of her cotton candy pink sneakers. "Because plastic is forever!"

"That's right. Plastic isn't biodegradable, so it pollutes the water for a long, long time. It can also make wildlife very sick."

"We don't wanna make Octavia and Oliver sick!" the little girl piped up, giving the litter bug a healthy helping of side eye.

Sophie smiled. "We sure don't." She tucked the annoying strand of hair behind her ear. Again. "Now if any of you would like a chance to learn more about Oliver and Octavia and their otter family—"

"Can we, Mom? Can we?"

An indulgent chuckle rippled through the group.

"There's a visitors' center on the research pier and you can even purchase tickets for a boat ride out into the bay. Thanks for visiting Regency Bay and enjoy the rest of your stay." *Except for you, trash panda. You can hoof it right back to your car and get lost.*

"Excuse me?"

Here we go. Someone wants directions to something we just walked past. She plastered on a smile and turned. "Hi, how can I help you?"

Oh. It was the trash knight in shining armor. The one with the incredible eyes. And even better smile. Two of his bottom teeth were slightly crooked, but the tiny imperfection made him all the more appealing. *To other people.*

"I wondered if you could recommend a good place to get a cup of coffee?"

Close your mouth and stop drooling. "Dashwood's Diner or Lady Catherine's Coffee Bar."

The corner of his mouth quirked up in a grin. "The first is from *Sense and Sensibility* if I'm not mistaken, but I'm not sure about the second."

She shrugged. "I couldn't tell you, but all the shops have cards in their front windows explaining the derivation of their name."

"Wait—you live in a place like this and you're not an Austen afficionado?"

And so, it begins. "Nope. Not my thing."

He smirked. "You mean not your cup of tea?"

Oddly, the stupid joke she'd heard about a zillion times didn't irritate her quite so much this time. "Bonnets and balls and tea parties do nothing for me. I read whatever was assigned in school then forgot all about it."

"You want to join me for a cup of coffee? You could tell me what kind of things you do enjoy reading."

Artistic and he reads? This could be interesting. Yeah...except for the part where you're a local and he's a summer guy. "Thanks. You're very kind, but I have to

3

get back to the office."

"Right. You're also the mayor."

"Where are my manners?" She extended her hand "Sophie Bennet, mayor of Regency Bay."

His hand was larger than hers, and surprisingly warm. "Sam Trowbridge. Roving photographer."

"Nice to meet you. And thanks for not making one of the standard jokes about my name."

He winked. "I wouldn't dream of annoying you. Wouldn't want your deputy to write me a ticket."

You're not annoying me…and that's the problem… She gave herself a mental shake. *What's a couple minutes conversation?* "Are you professional?" She nodded toward his camera. "That's quite a rig."

He fished a business card out of the back pocket of his beat-up denim shorts. "Professional. I'm here doing background work for a movie project."

Dammit. I knew he was too good to be true. "Well, I mustn't keep you from your, uh, background-ing." *Does he look disappointed? Stop it. You just met.*

"Well, maybe another time. I'm here all summer."

She glanced at the card—Pemberley Films—and stuffed it in her pocket. "Maybe." *Nope. Never. Summer flings never end well.*

****

Sophie ambled back toward the town hall with her Margaret's Maps tour guide vest folded over her arm. A town crew touched up the white paint on the bandstand, draping red, white, and blue bunting along the railing. Shopkeepers made final adjustments to their window displays—piles of adorable plush otter toys, new editions of the town's guidebook, and enticing bins of colorful fresh saltwater taffy. Regency Bay's roots as a posh resort town went back over a century. It occupied that sweet spot, just far enough from San Francisco to attract visitors looking for a quiet seaside experience, but close enough to the major transportation hub.

Damn, I wish I had coffee. With or without a side order of handsome photographer. I've got a pile of crap on my desk from that real estate developer, the Fourth of July plans to finalize, and I need to check the tour schedule for tomorrow...

Wilfred, or Wilf to a select few including Sophie, chatted with Deputy Bonnie as Sophie pushed through the salt-stained double doors. Balding, wearing wire framed glasses that slipped down his nose, Wilf was the town clerk and had been for as long as anyone could remember. His vast paunch testified to his fondness for the delights of the local sweet shops,

"You have two messages from that real estate fellow and one complaint from a disgruntled litter bug."

Wilf occupied a large desk organized with labeled plastic trays and file folders. The space to the left of his keyboard was clear except for a legal pad and pen. A desk for the deputy on duty, in this case, Bonnie, dominated the other half of the room. An open box of taffy and a voodoo doll of a man in a business suit vied for space with the standard computer monitor, a second for the traffic and safety cameras, and since it was Monday, a single travel cup.

Sophie took the three little pink slips and dropped them into the paper recycling bin next to Wilf's workstation. Her gaze drifted to her favorite thing about town hall—the series of framed photos depicting more than a century of beach goers and boardwalk strollers. The one from around 1900 fascinated her as a child. Her mom had explained that no, those ladies in long skirts and stiff shirtwaists weren't in costume—that's how people dressed for the beach back then.

Bonnie perched on the corner of the desk, ignoring Wilf's raised eyebrow. "Now that you've taken care of business, tell us all about the hottie."

"Nothing to tell. He's a summer guy taking pictures for some film project."

"But he's hot! And he picks up trash other people fling around."

"And he's a summer guy. As in, leaving in a few weeks."

"As in, here for a few weeks,"

Wilf leaned back in his wooden desk chair, which creaked alarmingly, and folded his hands on his ample stomach. "A lot can happen in a few weeks."

"Yeah, especially during tourist season. I don't have time to fool around with a summer guy."

Bonnie snapped her gum and blew a frizzy light brown curl out of her face. "You could do with a bit of fooling around, honey."

Sophie leveled a glare at Bonnie. "Mayor. Responsibilities."

"Pretty young lady. Summer," Wilf retorted. "You've hardly dated in all the time I've known you. Which, in case you've somehow forgotten, is your entire life."

"For very good reasons."

Wilf pursed his lips. "No one is asking you to select china patterns with this—or any other—young man. Just spend a little time together and see what happens."

She stooped and kissed the top of his bald head. "You old charmer. The last thing I need on my plate is a broken heart."

Bonnie blew a sticky pink bubble, which promptly popped. "Girl, you take things too seriously. There is nothing wrong with a little adult recreation. It doesn't have to be about forever."

"Uh-huh. I'll remind you of that come September when you're weeping into your third margarita because what's-his-face went back to Massachusetts."

"Finn. His name is Finn. He's a serious researcher and Regency Bay is a unique biological community. Whatever that means. He's not going anywhere."

Sophie waved a hand at the pair of them. "I'll be in my office hiding from real estate developers and litter bugs."

"And hot photographers?"

Chapter Two

Late Tuesday morning, Sam Trowbridge parked on a bench to check over his footage. The boardwalk was fascinating—all cute clapboard sided shops sporting striped awnings and signs painted with old-fashioned curlicue lettering. There was a refreshing lack of massage parlors, noisy arcades, and tattoo shops. It would make a fantastic backdrop for a historical film. Flags snapped in the fresh, clean breeze. He'd slept like a log every night since he arrived.

He looked up and spied a familiar slim redhead strolling the boardwalk. Her muscular legs and trim figure spoke of a lifetime swimming and walking beside the ocean. And biking—he'd seen her chaining a bicycle to the rack outside town hall. Not that he'd been on the lookout for her. Much.

He hurried to catch up with her. *Gotta keep on the mayor's good side if I wanna make this project happen. The fact that she has beautiful brown eyes, and a quirky smile has no bearing on my motives. Riiiiight...*

She stooped and petted a mackerel tabby who rubbed around her ankles. She offered it bits of fried goodness from a cardboard boat. He couldn't resist snapping a picture before he spoke.

"Keeping up with all your constituents?"

Sophie fed the kitty one last bite of her lunch, then stood. "Hey, I need every vote I can get."

" 'Cuz this is one of the toughest races on the west coast?"

" 'Cuz this is my home, and I care about what happens to it." She popped a fry into her mouth.

"How does one get to be mayor of a town like this, if you don't mind my asking?"

Her eyes narrowed and two spots of color blazed through her freckles. "By 'a place like this' I'm going to assume you mean 'such a wonderful, unique town.' "

Whoops. "Well, yes. That's exactly what I meant. Where else can you find this mix of Jane Austen and cutting-edge conservation?"

Her shoulders dropped and he released a long, slow breath.

"I have a degree in environmental science. The proposal to bring in a pair of otters to help rebalance the kelp bed was my senior project."

"Impressive."

She shrugged. "Impressive enough to be the youngest person named to the town council and the youngest elected mayor."

"And a tour guide?"

"Small town. Everyone wears lots of hats." She snuck a sidewise glance at him. "What about you? What are you keen about?"

"Telling unique stories. Like a grand old resort town making a comeback because of a family of otters." He fell into step beside her. "You don't think a film about Oliver and Octavia and everything you've achieved here would be good for your town?"

Sophie huffed out a breath. "We've had a couple of the big nature groups film documentaries here. Those generated some good attention for the town, but we have

9

to be careful not to overload our resources."

"The fancy water treatment plant doesn't compensate?"

She looked at him sharply.

"What? I listened to your tour." *Because you're pretty and funny and passionate about your town and your otters and—*

And he almost missed when she detoured over to a bin marked "compost" and deposited her used napkins and cardboard boat.

"It's complicated. Any new construction has to use green building methods—everything energy and water efficient, plus we try to preserve the aesthetic of the town."

He glanced around at the clapboard buildings. The tallest structures were the shingled towers of the big hotel where he was staying and a church spire. "It's beautiful here. And even if you didn't want to host a full movie production, this would be the perfect place to do some background shots for something historical. The last thing you'd want here is a concrete block of a big box store or a glass office tower. It would ruin the entire character of the place."

"Tell that to—"

He cocked his head curiously.

Sophie waved a hand. "Never mind. Anyway, there's also the historic buildings to consider. The four major hotels are over a century old. They were rebuilt with new plumbing and electricity after the 1906 earthquake, but it's all incredibly antiquated now."

That explains all the creaks and groans from the pipes when I shower.

"There're rules about retrofitting historic buildings.

The more people in town, the more water and electricity gets used, the more sewage goes into the system, and the harder it is to enforce the recycling regulations—as you saw yesterday."

"But wouldn't a nice family feel good movie increase your tourism revenue?"

"Mixed blessing. We got a lot of government funding to reclaim the bay, but it's based on us doing our part to maintain it. If we renege, a ton of bills come due."

A girl strolling on the boardwalk caught his eye. Her high-waisted floral print gown and parasol were a startling contrast to the swarm of shorts and flip-flops. "Isn't it a little early for Halloween?" He snapped a quick picture.

Sophie snorted. "I can see you're new around here. Vintage seaside resort full of Austen place names? We're a cosplayer and reenactor's dream. In fact, there's a convention in a couple of weeks, then a Regency romance writers retreat two weeks later. We even have a stable offering horse and carriage rides. You can book a carriage instead of a limo for special events. They also conduct seasonal tours of the town."

"I only understood about half the words you said." He snapped another shot of Sophie, paused resting her hand on the wooden rail, gazing out over the narrow expanse of sandy beach dotted with colorful umbrellas. "Maybe we could have a drink, and you could translate for me?"

A hint of pink stained her freckled cheeks. "Persistent, aren't you?"

He shrugged.

"Look, I'm flattered, but while you might be on vacation, it's the middle of the workday for me. I can't just go for a drink."

"Hey, I'm working, too, you know. Ice cream? Soda? Ice cream soda?"

She raised her hands in surrender. "Okay, okay—you win. Ice cream cone, but only because Sebastian's is right there." She checked her watch. "I have an hour before the final Fourth of July meeting, and I need to check in with my staff before it starts."

He trailed after her to a cute little shop with a pink and white striped awning shading the walk-up window.

****

Will you get hold of yourself? Summer guy. Bad news. No matter how appealing the package…

And it was appealing. He had the sort of body toned by frequent activity—not hours spent in a gym cultivating vanity muscles—exactly her type. And her fingers itched to discover if his hair was as soft as it looked.

"Your usual, Sophie?" the kid behind the counter asked.

"Please."

"And you, sir?"

"I'll have whatever she's having," Sam replied, reaching for his wallet.

"You got it. Two double dip mint chip waffle cones coming up." He stepped away from the window, returning scant moments later with two enormous cones and a huge grin plastered on his face. "Mac says these are on the house."

Sophie grabbed one of the cones and a couple of the compostable bamboo paper napkins. *I see the rumor mill—AKA Bonnie—arrived before me.* "Tell her thanks."

Sam dropped a ten in the tip bucket and took the other cone. "That's very kind."

She took a chomp of the top scoop of ice cream, letting the cool minty goodness slide down her throat.

"How the heck do I eat this without it dripping everywhere?" He licked an errant drip from the side of his hand.

"Rapidly. Trust me, it's not a problem." She'd eaten almost down to the edge of the cone. *Gobbling...so ladylike. Eh...I'm not looking to impress anyone. And this is too good to let it melt.*

He took a large bite. "This is great." He took another bite, chewed, and swallowed as they strolled toward town hall. "So...reenactors? I know what actors are, but what are reenactors?"

She crunched a bite of waffle cone. "Living history enthusiasts," she mumbled around her mouthful of crunchy sweet goodness, patting her mouth with a napkin. "They read everything—history, biography, books about textiles. Hell, some of them can give museum curators a run for their money. Their outfits are historically correct, right down to the underwear. A lot of it's even hand sewn." She eyed Sam out of the corner of her eye. Was he interested in this?

"They sound fascinating. Will I be able to meet any of those folks?"

She nodded. "Sure, if you're around. They're cool about talking to people and sharing what they know. But please ask permission if you want them to pose for any particular shots—they're visitors, not theme park characters."

"Got it. I always carry standard release forms when I'm working." He took an awkward bite out of his cone and a small dollop of ice cream plopped onto the boardwalk. "Dammit." He groped in his pocket for a spare napkin.

"No worries." Sophie slapped a hand over her mouth to repress a wave of giggles as her friend the tabby cat and a half-grown black kitty appeared out of nowhere to lap up the rapidly melting treat.

"Are they strays?"

"Part of a managed colony. They're all fixed and looked after by a vet. They keep the rodent population under control."

"So, you don't have to put out poison?"

"Exactly." She'd eaten half of her cone, conveying it neatly into her mouth through long practice.

"That makes sense." He licked another drip off his hand. "Okay, so reenactors are history people. What are cosplayers? I thought they were people who liked to dress up like cartoon characters?"

"Some of them do. And some of them like to recreate costumes from TV and movies. There's been a few big budget Regency-ish productions in recent years with lots of fans. They can be as enthusiastic about what they do as the history people. Just don't mix the two groups together!" She dropped her sticky napkins in a compost bin outside town hall. "This is me."

A framed poster displaying the Fourth of July schedule of events stood beside the double doors and a small glass enclosed case held event fliers so they wouldn't blow away. The bunting draped on the second floor balcony rustled in the breeze.

Sam still chomped on the end of his cone, trying to keep ahead of the drips. He had a smudge of pale green ice cream at the corner of his mouth, and she clenched her hand in her pocket to repress the impulse to wipe it off.

"Right. Important mayor stuff."

"Meeting with the police and fire chiefs to finalize the plans for the Fourth of July parade."

" 'Cuz that's so very Regency?"

" 'Cuz that's so very small town. You should come." *Why the hell did I invite him? Do not encourage the summer guy! You know better.* "Make sure you grab a copy of the town calendar. There's lots of great photo ops."

"I will. See you around, Mayor Sophie."

****

The U.S. and California state flags fluttered as Sophie shut the door to town hall. Her official portrait and the plaque listing the current town council members framed her office door. Wilf, as usual, was the epitome of summer business casual in his short sleeved button down shirt and suspenders. Bonnie was…well…Bonnie, snapping her gum and filing her nails. At least the voodoo doll wasn't visible.

"Woo-hoo! Ice cream with the hottie. You go, girl."

She glared at Bonnie. "Don't you have a boardwalk to patrol?"

Wilf turned from his computer and handed her messages. "After the Fourth of July meeting, we need to go over your schedule. You have invitations from the organizers of several of the big weekend events, including at least two—"

"Nooooooo…"

"—two for which you should have an escort."

"Not gonna happen."

"And perhaps even a new gown?"

"Definitely not."

"And Darrell is waiting in your office."

She scrunched her eyes shut. *Dammit, I should have taken Sam up on his offer of a drink.* She shoved a few stray wisps of hair behind her ears and tugged her shirt straight. Sucking in a deep breath, she walked across the lobby to her office. She glanced at her official portrait for reassurance and stepped inside.

Darrell Masterson rose from the guest chair, impeccable as always in a tailored three-piece suit, silk tie, and every hair on his head carefully styled in place. "Good afternoon, Sophie." His flat dark eyes had all the appeal of a visiting shark.

"Mr. Masterson, what can I do for you today?"

He extended a hand that had never done an honest day's work. "Darrell, please."

She shook his hand for a scant two seconds, then stalked around her desk and settled into her chair. "Mr. Masterson."

He sighed, gaze wandering from her untucked shirt and shorts to the neatly rolled flags standing in the corner next to the teetering stacks of boxed event fliers. "Mayor Bennet, I wonder if you might have a word with the management of the Delaford?"

"About what?"

"They're refusing to extend my contract for the meeting room, not to mention my own accommodations."

"I see." She leaned back in her chair. "This sounds like a matter for the hotel management. I don't have a say in how private businesses conduct their affairs."

"But you're the mayor."

"Yup. Not a hotel owner. So sorry I can't help you.

Perhaps one of the other hotels?" *Lotsa luck.*

Darrell's lips thinned, avoiding a frown by a narrow margin. "The other hotels also claim to be sold out."

"Well, it is our high season. We have events booked every weekend through Labor Day. Some of those groups are long-standing customers who return each summer. They're part of the Regency Bay family."

"As I clearly, am not."

She spread her hands and offered a half shrug. "I'm sure one of the hotels out on the thruway would be happy to accommodate you. Doesn't your company own a couple of them?"

"We both know relocating outside of town would serve no purpose."

"Mr. Masterson—"

"Darrell."

"Mr. Masterson, I can't ask a private business to break a contract with a long-standing guest for you."

"And even if you could, you wouldn't."

"Correct."

He steepled his hands. "Tell me, how long do you think this town can continue on the way it is?"

"We've been doing fine for well over a century."

"Yes, I can tell by the water pressure in my hotel room. Or the way the Netherfield sheds roof shingles every time there's a storm. The Northanger Holdings proposal—"

"Would change the entire character of the town, void our government agreements, raise taxes for local residents through the roof, and dispossess an unacceptable number of businesses and homeowners."

"Our proposal would revitalize Regency Bay and provide hundreds of jobs."

"Minimum wage jobs for big corporations. If our residents wanted that lifestyle, they wouldn't live here. No thank you."

He rose, collecting a designer leather briefcase that looked like it cost a month's rent. "You know, Sophie, it only takes is one bad storm to put one of these old hotels out of commission for a season. What then? Can any of these businesses afford to lose a whole summer's income? It's just a matter of time."

"Most things are, Mr. Masterson."

"Well, I'll see myself out." He didn't bother to close the door.

Sophie slumped in her seat. *The hell of it is, he's right. All it'll take is one bad season and one hotel caving to their proposal.*

Chapter Three

Sam had to admit, for a town full of British literary references, Regency Bay served up the Fourth of July to pure small-town American perfection. Red, white, and blue bunting draped all the buildings along Austen Boulevard and flags flew from the wrought iron lamp posts. Granted, he had no clue if they were Regency appropriate, but they were cute—like something out of one of those British costume flicks. The salt-sweet scent of kettle corn drifted on the breeze and the screeching of gulls fighting over dropped French fries assaulted his ears.

He'd staked out a vantage point on the balcony of town hall, the terminus of the parade route. He'd gotten some long shots of the entire parade, then switched lenses and focused on individual groups as they completed the march. Vehicles turned off onto the side street that ran behind the big hotels, while marching bands and other pedestrian groups continued onto the boardwalk. *Thank God all the bands transitioned to a group rendition of Yankee Doodle once they hit the boardwalk...although it may take me the rest of the summer to lose the ear worm.* He stuck his little finger in his ear and wiggled it a bit, as if he could dislodge the offending tune.

A vintage pickup truck sporting a glossy sea-green paint job hauled one last float to the finish line. A pair of actors who must be approaching heat stroke in their furry brown otter costumes clambered out, followed by a smiling and waving Sophie. She wore a sleeveless blue dress printed with whimsical otters. It suited her, hugging her curves while still being perfectly appropriate. She looked cool and confident, shaking hands and speaking with people as she made her way through the crowd to a small podium. Feedback squawked from the speakers, then she began her speech.

"Thank you everyone for coming out to join us on this beautiful Fourth of July. We're looking forward to another amazing summer here in Regency Bay. Whether you come for the themed events or the science, we're so pleased to welcome everyone—"

"Mayor Bennet, how do you respond to claims the representative from Northanger Holdings is being, and I quote 'run out of town?' " a weaselly looking man clutching a notebook and chewing the stump of an unlit cigar interrupted.

Irritated mutterings and scattered boos ran through the crowd.

"With laughter?" Sophie replied, still keeping her cool. "Northanger Holdings has maintained a presence in one of the local hotels since January, as well as being guests at several town meetings, and getting quite a bit of coverage in your paper, Marcus. Residents have had plenty of time to review the facts and form their own opinions."

"Residents, yes, but how can Northanger Holdings be expected to connect with visitors if their representative is told he should seek lodging at a hotel outside the town limits?"

Well, this is getting ugly.

Kids wriggled impatiently, itching to head to the amusement pier or the otter visitor center. People wandered off down the boardwalk, away from the drama.

Sophie pressed her lips together for a long moment before speaking. "Okay, you're mixing several different issues into one argument. First, while we welcome and value our seasonal guests, they don't live here. They don't pay property taxes or send their kids to school in Regency Bay. They simply aren't entitled to the same level of input into how we live and do business as the folks who live here." She raised her hand when it looked as though he was about to interrupt. Again.

"And before you get started about how tourist dollars are the lifeblood of a town like ours, I'd like to remind you there's a little thing called the internet. Every guest who books a vacation and every organization that plans an event here has done their research. If they wanted to stay at a full-service resort or a theme park, they would. But they choose to come here.

"They read the publicly posted information about the high season and blackout dates and our environmental awareness policies, and they still choose to come here. Several of our major events return year after year, filling our hotels to capacity. They come because they love our town." She paused, smiling at the crowd. "And we're so very glad to welcome them. So, without further ado, everyone be sure to grab a schedule of events. Go visit Oliver and Octavia, ride the carousel, or decide between the clambake or the barbeque for dinner. Be sure to join us back here at nine p.m. for the drone light show."

She nodded to someone and the bands reprised Yankee Doodle, much too loud for Marcus to get in another word as she descended from the podium to hearty applause.

Sam packed his gear, slung his bag over his shoulder, and headed down to the boardwalk.

****

Even at street level, he easily picked Sophie out of the crowd. Her blue dress and vivid hair drew him like a beacon. She stooped for a picture with the cute little girl from the tour who was so enamored of Oliver and Octavia. However, as he made his way through the crowd, he noticed her smile seemed a trifle forced—and was she a bit pale? Her friend the deputy hovered nearby, increasing his concern. He applied his elbows and excuse mes a little more forcefully and pushed through the crowd.

He caught Sophie's arm and brushed a friendly kiss on her cheek. "Madame Mayor, great parade!"

"Thanks. Did you get some good shots?"

"Tons. It'll take me a while to sort and edit them." He leaned closer. "Are you okay? You look like you could use some shade and water."

An obnoxiously loud voice overrode whatever reply was on Sophie's lips. "See, this is what happens when voters put their confidence in such a young candidate. Her social life takes precedence over important town events."

Sophie stiffened and leaned away from him.

"Excuse me, Marcus, is it? The mayor and I have a conference scheduled. I'm working on a film project which will highlight her environmental policies and how they generate revenue for the town. If you'll excuse us, I know how valuable the mayor's time is."

"Oh, and Marcus?" the deputy added sweetly,

"Don't even think about lighting up until you're clear of the boardwalk."

He glared at her but replaced his battered old lighter in his pocket and stomped away clenching the unlit cigar between his teeth.

Sam nodded and steered Sophie toward the diner, which promised seats and air conditioning. And a public venue, effectively shutting down the idea he and Sophie were on a date, however enticing the idea might be.

A waitress on roller-skates guided them to a window table, where Sophie could wave to her constituents. She returned moments later carrying two glasses of ice water and a plate of fries. "Mom says it's gonna be a long hot day and you need to mind your electrolytes."

Sophie popped a fry into her mouth. "Tell her thank you, Jenny."

In keeping with the ruse of a conference, he pulled out his camera and passed it to Sophie so she could see the shots he'd gotten. "Look, I don't mean to be in your business, but are you okay? I mean, are you diabetic or something? You looked kinda shaky."

She sipped her water. "No, nothing like that. It's just…I was never the cheerleader type, you know? I never wanted to be the center of attention. I learned to speak about subjects I'm passionate about—"

"Like your town and the environment?"

She nodded, nibbling on another fry. "But I have to psych myself up to it and have a handle on what I'm going to say."

"And not be interrupted by some jerk. Who was he? It seemed a bit…intense."

She snorted into her water glass. "A bit something. Marcus runs the local conservative newspaper."

"Let me guess—he's not a fan of the youngest mayor in the town's history, who also happens to be a woman?"

"Yup. I should have kept it together better. Dammit." She winced and crumpled a paper napkin.

He helped himself to one of her fries, which were the perfect blend of crispy and salty. "Hey, I think you did fine."

She shook her head. "The laughter comment. I shouldn't have given him an opening. He'll spin it into something awful, you'll see."

"I might, if I believed in supporting obviously biased journalism."

"I may not support him, but I have to read what he prints. I don't have a choice in the matter." She perused the pictures on his camera.

He shifted in his seat. *I hope she's not creeped out by how many are of her.*

"These are amazing. Even if the film project doesn't pan out, I bet you could do a coffee table book or something."

"Thank you. But what was that nonsense about someone being run out of town?"

Sophie rolled her eyes, looking a bit brighter for the fries she'd eaten. "There's a rep from a company called Northanger Holdings who's had a meeting room at the Delaford for the last few months. He was informed very clearly in writing when he booked that his reservation couldn't be extended past July fifteenth because of a longstanding event which has a pre-existing contract."

"So was I, but I've been helping the research team and one of them—Finn? He put in a good word with the boarding house he's staying at, the yellow one with all the porches."

"Barton Cottage."

"That's the one. I'll be moving over there."

She looked up with a delicate blush staining her cheeks. "So, you're staying?"

"I am. At least until Labor Day."

She dropped her gaze back to her plate for a moment, then peeked up through her lashes. "I'm glad."

Those two small words warmed him more than the bright summer sunshine. "So am I."

Chapter Four

Sophie stepped inside the questionably air-conditioned town hall Monday morning and shoved her sunglasses on top of her head. The ancient AC units wheezed and buzzed. *Please, let them last the summer.* Wilf slid a tall paper cup of something cold and sweet her way without looking up from the morning papers. She grabbed the cup and took a deep, fortifying gulp. *Blessed caffeine. And also, sugar.*

"Okay, how bad is it?"

Wilf cleared his throat ostentatiously. " 'Mayor considers lack of available lodging during high season a laughing matter.' "

"Freakin' Marcus," Bonnie muttered from her desk. "I shoulda wrote him a ticket."

Wilf looked over the top of the paper. "For what?"

"Being Marcus."

"Sorry. He caught me off guard." Sophie took another slurp of her iced coffee concoction. "What else?"

"A full-page ad from Northanger Holdings. 'Last chance to weigh in on our development plans.' "

"Proposed development plans. There's a difference." She drained her cup and looked mournfully at the empty bottom. "Anyone reporting anything non-offensive?"

"The Clarion has full coverage of the artists registered for the sand sculpture event and pictures of the prize winners from last year."

"Good."

"We need to answer those event invitations. I've taken the liberty of clearing your tour schedule for the days in question."

" 'Taken the liberty'? Have you been watching British TV shows again?"

Wilf merely raised an eyebrow. "Now, about the costume balls—"

"Wait—balls? Plural?"

"Last time I checked, three was plural."

Sophie flopped into Wilf's guest chair and buried her face in her hands. "Not three of them…"

"One for the cosplay event, one for the reenactors' event, and the romance writers decided to join the trend this year. Three. And you need to make an appearance at each, preferably in costume and with an escort."

"Great excuse for a hot date with a hot photographer."

Sophie raised her head and glared at Bonnie.

"Don't give me that look. I know he's in town for the whole summer. Finn helped him reserve a room at Barton Cottage for the rest of the season."

"And what if he isn't interested in dressing up in full costume in the middle of summer and making a fool of himself?"

"But he is. He told Finn he was looking forward to the full Regency Bay experience. He's even been asking around for a place he can rent an outfit."

"Is there no such thing as privacy?"

Bonnie snapped her gum. "In a town this size? Hell, no." She scooted her wheeled office chair out from behind her desk. "Look, no one's expecting you to marry the guy, all right? Just ask him to the first ball and see what happens. If you really can't stand one another, you don't ask him out again. Although I don't think that'll be an issue."

"It's evident to anyone who sees you together that you're well suited," Wilf agreed.

"Anyone? Who's anyone?"

Bonnie ticked off names on her fingers. "Jenny at the diner, the new kid at Sebastian's, hell, even Marcus."

"Not to mention us," Wilf added, leaning back in his chair and folding his hands on his stomach.

Sophie flung up her hands in surrender. "Fine. I'll ask him. Are you people happy now?"

****

Two hours later, Sophie sat slumped behind her desk, sorting through the contents of her in-box. Wilf weeded it down as best he could. She knew he did, but sometimes the nonsense that found its way to her desk astounded her.

Final invoice for the drone light show. Okay fine. That belonged there. She winced at the number and slid it underneath the bottom of the pile. Hopefully Marcus wouldn't get wind of it.

Complaints from Darrell about the management of the Delaford. Complaints from the Delaford about Darrell. *And this is my problem because why?*

And whyyyyyy did I ever agree to ask a guy I barely know out on a date? Especially to a fancy event I don't even want to attend?

Although it could be interesting. Guys in Regency clothes fell into one of two categories—those who looked like total dorks in Halloween costumes, and the ones who could carry off the breeches and tailcoat.

Which category would Sam be? He looked awfully good in shorts…and not that she'd ever admit it to Bonnie, but…"hottie" was pretty accurate.

An offer to borrow a gown from one of the convention vendors. Enough already, Wilf. She paused in the act of tossing it in the recycle bin. *If I invite Sam, maybe it's time for a new look. One with less memories attached.* She smoothed the paper and tucked it into her bag.

Her phone chirped from somewhere in the chaos. She rooted around her desk for a few minutes, finally found it at the bottom of her bag and opened a text from Bonnie.

—Lunchtime!—

—Guess who's checking out the food carts on the amusement pier?—

Followed by emojis of hotdogs, fries, and a camera. Sophie rolled her eyes. The phone chirped again.

—You know I'll find out if you don't ask him.—

****

As usual, the minute Sophie stepped outside, the stiff sea breeze whipped a few strands of hair loose from her braid. She brushed them aside as she headed for the amusement pier, waving to a tour group and darting out of the path of a couple of bicycle cabs. Calliope music and the shouts of happy kids competed with the crash of the surf and the screech of gulls.

Of course, Sam was right in the middle of things, capturing every bit of the joyous color and activity on film. Those faded denim shorts fit him quite well, and a tank top showed off his nicely toned arms. He spotted her and grinned, snapping a picture or two.

Great. I'm all windblown. And why are my palms so

sweaty?

"Sophie, I hoped I'd run into you. Care to join me for lunch?"

"Sure. Why not? A girl's gotta eat. Or so people keep telling me." She clenched her hand in her pocket, resisting the urge to brush a stray lock of hair away from his eyes.

"I planned on sampling the culinary delights of the local food carts. Judging from the way the gulls keep trying to steal them, I'm thinking the hotdogs are a good bet?"

"And you'd be right."

They purchased footlong hotdogs and chilled bottles of water from a cart shaded by a red striped awning, then found a table in a sheltered pavilion.

"No tours today?" Sam asked.

Sophie chewed and swallowed her mouthful of hotdog. "Today's an office day. I need to follow up on the Fourth of July paperwork and final numbers, and make sure everything's set for next weekend."

"The sand sculptures, right?"

She nodded. "Mm-hmm."

"The Monday after, I have to switch hotels because of one of the Regency costume thingies."

Sophie patted her lips with a napkin and took a sip of water. "The cosplay convention. It's been around for a while, but it's exploded the last couple of years because of that new TV show. They've blocked every single room and event space at all four hotels. Some overflow guests are staying at hotels out on the thruway. You were lucky to get a room at the boarding house. They usually cater to the visiting research teams."

She took another bite of her lunch and caught Sam

grinning across the table. "What?"

He reached over and dabbed a bit of something from the corner of her mouth with a napkin.

Right. I am a classy lady.

He somehow managed to convey his own condiment-laden monstrosity into his mouth without a drip.

"I was warned the accommodations would be quite different from the Netherfield, but honestly, I don't mind. I only sleep and shower there, so it's not like I'm missing anything."

Shower. The word conjured all sorts of visions she really shouldn't be entertaining while out in public. She cleared her throat. "The boarding houses are clean and safe, just not fancy."

"So, like being in a college dorm again?"

"Well, a little better. You'll have your own bathroom, anyway."

"So, the guy from…Angry-something—what's his problem?"

She sighed and crumpled her used napkin into the empty cardboard sleeve from her hotdog. "Northanger Holdings. It's a finance company that's trying to buy out the boardwalk hotels."

"Why?"

"They want to build an all-inclusive resort."

"And that's bad?"

"Very bad. They've had a rep on-site at the Delaford for a few months now. His models and artwork look very charming, until you realize what he's proposing is a theme park caricature of our town—it replaces all the family-owned businesses on the boardwalk with mass-produced copies."

31

Sam looked around at the lovingly maintained vintage amusements on the pier. "The carrousel is stunning. I love all those tiny little mirrors. And the colors of the Ferris wheel cars remind me of taffy or maybe sherbet…something sweet. The calliope music is a nice touch."

"It's a fine line to walk. Guests want rides, but we want to keep the feel vintage, not loud and screamy with flashing lights."

"I've only been here a couple of weeks, but I like it here. This town has charm and character. I'd hate to see it replaced by prepackaged plastic."

"It's not just the look of things. The facilities necessary to support the increased number of rooms and amenities would require leveling several neighborhoods. So that's longtime residents losing their businesses, jobs, and homes. And don't get me started on the environmental impact."

Sam reached across the table and took her hand. "Hey—I didn't mean to upset you. It sounds like your neighbors have spoken and given this guy his walking papers."

She blinked to clear a shimmer of imminent tears. "Sorry. It's just—"

"You love your town. I get it." He squeezed her fingers.

She sucked in a deep breath. "Darrell—the rep—he keeps reminding me all it takes is one bad storm, one bad season, and someone will cave in to their offer. Once they get a foothold—"

"But he's leaving, right? Out of sight, out of mind?"

"I wish I had the luxury." She gently withdrew her hand and rubbed her face.

"Look, I understand you're the mayor and it's your job to worry about this town, but it sounds like the evil real estate guy is on his way out, and you've got a wonderful summer planned. I'd love it if you'd show me around the town—not just the big things, but your favorite places."

She chuckled ruefully and blew the offending strands of hair out of her eyes. "I'd like that, too. In fact—and you can totally feel free to say no, because I know it's not for everyone—but the cosplay event includes a ball."

"What, like in a fairy tale?"

"More like in a Jane Austen novel. In costume and everything. Since it's such a big event, I have to make an appearance."

"And since it's a ball, it might be handy to bring your own dancing partner?"

"Yeah."

His answering grin warmed her more than the bright noon sunshine.

"I'd love to."

Chapter Five

Sophie skimmed through her email, waiting for Bonnie to emerge from the dressing room of Phoebe's Finery. She was almost to the end of the latest sparring match between Darrell Masterson and the management of the Delaford when the door clicked open, and Bonnie stepped out in a rustle of stiff, lime-green satin. A headband covered in satin rosettes held her frizzy curls in some semblance of order. More rosettes trimmed the hem of the gown. Oddly enough, the high-waisted, puff-sleeved confection suited her.

Sophie winced. "Did that color even exist back then?"

Bonnie shrugged, craning her neck to see the back of the dress in the mirror. "Who cares? This for fun. Anyway, I've seen it on TV, so there's gonna be lots of other people wearing it."

"Are you gonna rent it for the season?"

"I haven't decided yet. I adore the color, but it's fun to wear a different dress to every party."

No, it's fun to avoid every party all together.

"If I have a good time, I'll probably want to wear it again. If I don't, well…"

"Plenty of other researchers in the sea?"

"Sophie, there's nothing wrong with a little variety. But Finn and I are having a lot of fun so far. There's nothing wrong with enjoying a good thing while you've got it—or leaving behind things you don't enjoy. Like a dress full of bad memories." She stepped away from the mirrors and grabbed Sophie's hand, trying to tug her to her feet. "Come on—live a little. At least look at a new dress. You've been wearing your blue silk since college."

Sophie didn't budge. "And how many times a year do I wear it?"

"As few as you can get away with. But you're the mayor. People notice what you wear."

Did they ever. The cosplay people think my blue gown is too boring. The history people think it's too off the rack. And the general public..."People look for things to comment on, like how much I spend on things which are none of their business, like my clothes."

"Sophie, I love you, but you hang onto things too tightly. A summer guy broke your heart—way the hell back when you were in college. Years ago. Now come on and pick out a new dress—something you won't associate with what's his name dumping you at Christmas."

"Thanks so much for the reminder." *And it was two summer guys, even if the second wasn't quite as spectacular of a disaster—and I'm not about to remind her.*

"He was a jerk, and you give him way too much space in your head. Come on, new guy, new dress."

"As it happens...one of the convention vendors offered to loan me a gown for the ball."

"And will you take them up on it?"

The pale blue one with the lace is gorgeous. What would Sam think of it? "Maybe."

****

Sophie sat at the head of a table of hotel managers and public safety officers, leafing through proposed sand sculpture designs. She straightened the stack and passed it to her neighbor to peruse. "Most of these are fine. Wilf, please email the guy who wants to sculpt the mermaid and tell him he has to put a bra on her, would you?"

A wave of snickers and groans rippled around the table.

"How are we set for hotel rooms? I think you've all got weddings booked, in addition to the sand sculptors?"

Marge, the manager of the Delaford, straightened her glasses on her nose. "We do. Enough of the Fourth of July people are checking out to accommodate the new arrivals with no problem. Well, except my one major headache guest who thinks blackout periods don't apply to him."

"Told you not to rent to him," the assistant manager of the Norland remarked smugly.

"I needed the revenue. Besides, I didn't have a legitimate reason not to and I didn't feel like dealing with a nuisance lawsuit for discrimination."

Sophie leaned forward. "Did he threaten a suit?"

"Not in so many words, but he insinuated, and I didn't need the publicity or legal bills."

"Well, if he hassles you about leaving, he'll be in breach of contract."

"I just hope he goes quietly. I've got enough on my plate without formal eviction proceedings."

"Let me know how it goes." Sophie glanced around the table. "Anything else?"

Stan, the harbormaster, raised his hand deferentially. "I'm a little concerned about the latest weather reports."

"How bad?"

He flipped open a file folder and studied the pages inside. "Rain squalls. Maybe enough to put a damper on the festival."

"Enough to cause damage?" the owner of the Netherfield asked, running a finger under his collar to loosen it. "I just finished paying off the repairs from the big spring storm."

"It's not an exact science. You know that."

Sophie rapped her knuckles lightly on the tabletop. "Folks, whatever happens, we'll deal with it as a community, like we always do. The contest has a no refunds policy in place for a reason. Stan, please keep an eye on the forecast and let us know if we need to take any precautions. Anyone else?"

"Well, yes," Marge said, glancing around the table. "Do you think you could be a little more careful what you say to Marcus?"

"Who cares what his rag prints?" Stan scoffed. "He's always looking to pick a fight."

Marge raised a hand. "Now look, I don't like him any better than the rest of you, but this is the age of the internet, whether we like it or not. Anything a local paper prints ends up online one way or another. I know he's full of it, and I'm happy to see you dating a nice young man."

"I'm not—he's—we're not—"

Wilf spoke up. "Mr. Trowbridge is here doing photography for a potential film project. As for the…incident on the Fourth, it was a long week of event prep, everyone was tired, and Marcus was being Marcus."

Sophie flashed him a grateful look. "Yeah. I'll try to

have some Marcus-proof comments prepared for the other events." *About my wardrobe, personal finances, and non-existent social life.*

Marge caught her arm as the meeting broke up. "Honey, I'm just saying, if I was thirty years younger…" She winked and joined the group exiting the conference room.

Why does everyone think this is their business? I'm fine on my own.

****

The brass bell over the door clanked when Sam entered the Anchor on Wednesday evening. He shrugged out of his windbreaker and shook it outside the door before hanging it on one of the hooks beside the entrance. Unlike Almack's, the tourist bar on the boardwalk which boasted a curated selection of imported beer and wine and overpriced cocktails, the local pub served domestic beer, a few local wines, and hearty pub food. Even though he was a summer visitor, he'd made enough local connections to feel welcome. Usually.

Tonight, however, the standard cheerful wrangling about work and sports was replaced by a buzz of angry tension. He spotted Bonnie and Finn at the bar and took a seat on the next stool.

Bonnie looked over his shoulder. "I hoped you'd have Sophie with you. I'm not sure if she remembered to grab lunch today."

"Crap. If I'd known, I would have stopped by the office."

The gray-haired bartender glanced his way enquiringly, though without her usual affable smile.

"Burger and a beer, please."

She nodded, called his order to the cook, and

grabbed a beer from the cooler with an economy of motion that belied her apparent age and girth.

"Thanks, Daisy." He turned to Bonnie. "What's got everyone so uptight?"

She blew a curl out of her face. "Okay, you know the company that's trying to buy the boardwalk hotels?"

"Yes, Sophie told me. They want to build a fancy resort that would put a lot of folks out of their homes and businesses, right?"

"Yup." She stabbed the swizzle stick from her margarita into a bit of fruit and popped it into her mouth. "They own a big mall out on the thruway. Today they announced they're holding an indoor sand sculpture contest this weekend."

"Indoors? How do you host an indoor sand sculpture event?"

Finn leaned around Bonnie. "They build large box forms out of wood and haul in a load of sand. It's not such a big deal if you have the funds," he explained in his broad New England accent.

"Okay, but why?"

Daisy thumped the heavy ceramic plate containing his burger onto the bar top. "They're offering a free entry to anyone pre-registered for our event, which is in danger of being rained out. Plus, they have a big box home improvement store undercutting the prices at Benjamin's for plastic buckets and such that sculptors use."

The man at the next stool slid a crumpled copy of Marcus's paper his way. "And they're offering discount tickets to their multiplex and indoor amusement park."

"So, they're setting up local merchants to take a fall if the town's event is called because of weather?" *Sophie must be losing her mind.* "How likely is that?"

"Well, the folks who come for the contest don't much care if they get wet," Finn said, "but if the surf is too heavy, the event may need to be canceled for safety. And if there's a hard enough downpour, it can damage the sculptures."

Sam took a bite of his burger and chewed. "That sucks." He dragged a fry through a drip of ketchup. "They threw all this together in two days?"

"Money talks," Bonnie muttered, picking up her drink and draining it.

Daisy collected the empty glass and wiped the wet ring from the bar top with a ragged towel. "The guy Marge was fool enough to rent to has had months to learn about the summer schedule and figure out ways to one-up us." She glanced at the TV set above the bar. "Speak of the devil."

A man in a three-piece suit and tie appeared on the TV screen, only to be greeted by a hail of crumpled napkins and straw wrappers. Daisy clicked off the set and turned, hands on her ample hips. "Which one of you lot just volunteered to sweep my floor?" She leveled a glare at a fellow at the end of the bar who froze in the act of reaching for a basket of popcorn.

"Sure thing, Daisy," he said ruefully, sliding down from his bar stool.

Sam turned back to Bonnie. "What about the cosplay event next week?"

She waved a hand dismissively. "The cosplay group's been coming here for years. Other hotels have tried to poach them, but they like it here. The Regency stuff's so popular right now, they're even talking about a second event for Halloween—a murder mystery game following clues through different shops along the boardwalk."

"That's great. So how does this ball work?"

"This one's pretty laid back. They'll do one or two set dances from the TV show, but then they switch to regular music. It's kinda like prom—a lot of the boardwalk stays open all night and people wander around in costume doing whatever."

"Set dances?"

Daisy removed his empty plate. "Like square dancing, but more formal. You can find videos online or a couple places in town offer classes."

"Huh. Maybe I should look into that."

Chapter Six

Rain plastered Sophie's hair against her scalp and a stiff breeze lashed the red No Swimming flags. The amusement pier stood silent and empty. It was hardly what she'd wished for Saturday of the sand sculpture festival, but as usual, the town pulled together. A lot of locals were out shopping on the boardwalk, bolstering sales from the guests who scurried from shop to shop.

Sam squelched up beside her, camera protected by a plastic cover. Instead of his usual cutoffs, he wore cargo shorts and a vest, pockets bulging with supplies, all covered by a clear plastic rain poncho. He looked dry and comfy, except for his soaked canvas tennis shoes.

While I look like a drowned rat. Not like it matters. I'm not in the market for a guy.

He nodded toward the sculptors hard at work on the beach. "They came."

A castle, a dragon, and a full-masted sailing ship slowly took form out on the beach. The fellow sculpting the mermaid had been firmly reminded to include a bra. Or clamshells. Anything to stave off a rant about public decency. A few artists huddled under golf umbrellas, working on fine details, but for the most part, the sculptors disregarded the weather.

"They did. They said they signed up to sculpt on a beach, not in a sandbox."

"But the boardwalk is losing foot traffic and

concession sales."

She shrugged, tucking a few stray strands of hair behind her ear. "Weather's gonna weather and there's nothing anyone can do about it. The shops and indoor dining will probably make their numbers. The weddings are indoors, so no one's losing income due to the rain."

"But the boardwalk is such a great backdrop for outdoor photos. It's a shame they'll miss out on those photo ops."

"Mixed blessing. People have a habit of overindulging at weddings. I'm happier when they don't go wandering near the beach after one too many. As long as the storm doesn't ratchet up to destructive levels, we're okay."

"The research pier is hopping."

"Oliver and Octavia are already wet. They don't care if it rains. Neither do the whales."

He brushed a lock of damp hair out of his eyes. "How's the idiot factor?"

"Not too bad. A couple of college kids needed a ticket and a fine to understand 'no swimming, beach closed' included them, but again, it's nothing Bonnie can't handle." She adjusted her soaked windbreaker.

"Have you been out here all day?"

"Pretty much. You?"

"Yeah. Finn and the guys took me out on the research boat. The baby otter is adorable."

"You saw the baby? I'm jealous." The wind picked up and she shivered. "They don't let me get close enough for good pictures."

Sam glanced at the solid gray mass of clouds. "How much longer are you gonna be out here?"

She checked her watch. "I can probably call it a day.

These guys will be packing it in soon."

"You didn't ride your bike in this, did you? I mean…I could give you a ride…"

She rolled her eyes. "I'm eco-friendly, not insane. I drove my truck today."

"Truck, huh? I didn't figure you for a truck girl."

"Sometimes I need to move lots of stuff. It's practical."

"I wondered about something."

"Such as?"

"Those vintage trucks in the parade, they're gorgeous, but aren't they awful gas guzzlers? It seems so out of character here."

"They would be, if they still had their original innards. We have a shop in town that specializes in resto-mods—restoring vintage cars so they look like they just rolled off the assembly line but rebuilding the insides with the latest technology. Those trucks you saw are all electric and produce minimal emissions. The one I drive used to be my grandpa's."

"Impressive, Madame Mayor."

"I try."

"I just leased my first EV. It's been a bit of a learning curve. "

"Hey, we all have to start somewhere." She bumped her shoulder against his and tapped her earpiece. "Bonnie, if there's nothing needing my attention, I'm signing off for the day."

"Nothing to report, boss. Have fun with the hottie."
Thank God, he didn't hear her.

"It's…a…getting a little soggy out here. How about some dinner? Nothing fancy just, you know—dry?"

Heat blossomed across her cheekbones. "I should

really—"

"Sophie, you need to eat. You've been out here getting rained on all day."

"Well—"

"We could go to the Anchor. Less prying eyes."

"Less" isn't "none." And I need a decent night's sleep to judge the contest tomorrow.

"Come on—you have to eat," Sam wheedled. "I'll show you the pictures I took of the baby."

She raised her hands in mock-surrender. "Okay, okay…the Anchor it is."

****

Mercifully, Daisy seated them in a quiet corner booth, as far as possible from the sports-ball-related mayhem surrounding the television. She didn't even scold them for dripping on her floor, just handed them two frayed old towels bearing the remains of long faded beer logos along with their menus.

Daisy returned a few minutes later and plunked two steaming mugs of coffee on their table. "Looks like the pair of you could do with something to warm you up. I made lobster mac and cheese today. This damn weather gets into my joints, and I wanted something nice and hot."

"Lobster mac and cheese sounds perfect, Daisy," Sophie replied, returning the menu she hadn't even opened.

"Two please," Sam added.

Sophie added sugar and cream to her coffee and took a long, fortifying sip. Warmth gradually spread through her body. *Damn, I must have been more chilled than I realized.*

Sam doctored his own mug and stirred it without

45

taking a drink. "Can I ask you something?"

"Sure."

He wrapped his hands around the thick ceramic mug, still not drinking. "This is gonna sound weirdly middle school, but I can't think of a better way to phrase it. I like you, Sophie, and sometimes, I think you like me, too, but other times you seem to be dodging me. I don't go where I'm not wanted. I'm not that egotistical. If you don't want me around, tell me."

"It's not quite so simple."

"Because you're the mayor? I can be discreet. And Sophie, I'm not just looking for—I mean if we were going to—we'd use protection. I'm not looking to complicate anyone's life, my own included."

She took another long sip of her coffee. "No. Not because of that, although I'm glad you're a responsible partner." She set her mug down with a thump, feeling heat creep up the back of her neck. "It's because I'm local and you're summer." *Dammit, where's the food? We need a distraction.*

"Okay? I don't understand what you mean. Please explain it to me." He reached across the table and took her hand. "Please."

Did he really mean it? She drew a deep breath to settle her racing heart. "This town…it's in my bones. I was born here, my folks grew up here, they run a hardware store that's been in the family for generations."

"I love how passionate you are about Regency Bay."

She looked down at the battered tabletop, scarred with chips and carved initials. "My first summer home from college, I met a guy." She met his gaze. "A summer guy. He was handsome and clever and really into conservation. And I fell for him, hook, line, and sinker. I believed him when he said a long-distance relationship was no big deal with email and video calls. And I believed him when he said he'd be back for the holiday break. I believed him when he said he needed to stop off at home to spend Christmas with his family, but he'd definitely be here for the New Year's Eve ball."

She dropped her gaze to the fascinating table. "I believed him, right until I got a text at five minutes past midnight saying he wasn't coming. He'd met someone at school and etcetera, etcetera."

Sam wrapped both hands around hers. "First, ouch. He sounds like a prize jerk."

The corner of her mouth ticked up slightly. "Bonnie prefers a different term."

"Having met Bonnie, I'm sure she does, but I was trying to be polite. Second, I'm not that guy. For one thing, I hope I'm a touch more mature than I was in college." He squeezed her hand gently. "Look, I'm not promising to marry you and settle down here forever. I'm saying I'd like to get to know you, and whatever does or does not happen, there will be a frank and open discussion, all right? Would you give me a chance?"

"I'd like to, if you can accept I might still get weirded out occasionally…I'm just…I'm not good at casual."

"I love how passionate you are about your town and your family and the environment."

"And everything I do tends to hit the news cycle around here, either officially or un."

"I've noticed, and I'm okay with it."

"If you're ever not okay with it, please promise me we'll talk about that too?"

"I promise."

"Okay then." She squeezed his hands. "I guess we're doing this."

****

Sam stood behind the police tape the following morning, photographing the impromptu press conference.

"Mayor Bennet," Marcus demanded, clutching his battered notebook, "can you tell us where you were last night when this terrible tragedy occurred?"

Sophie spoke directly into the mic. "The storm surge occurred around two o'clock this morning, so I was home asleep, like most other people. I answered the initial text from first responders at two fifty-two and arrived at town hall at about three thirty."

Sam panned around and captured images of the half-finished sand sculptures and scattered shingles. Gulls squabbled over the contents of a tipped over compost bin.

"What can you tell us about the deceased?"

The police chief leaned over and spoke into the mic. "Nothing at this time, pending notification of next of kin."

"And how do you answer concerns about crime during the high season? What are your plans for keeping our community safe?"

Sophie frowned and reclaimed the mic. "The safety of our community and our guests is always our first priority. However, there is no evidence of wrongdoing. At this time, the incident is being considered death by misadventure."

"Oh, so it's the victim's fault?"

"Marcus, cut the crap," someone called from the crowd, garnering scattered applause.

A reporter from the Clarion raised his hand. "Can you tell us what steps will be taken to repair the damage before next week's convention? It's a major source of revenue for many local businesses."

"It is, indeed, and we'll be ready for our guests. The damage appears to be mainly cosmetic, and the proprietors of Benjamin's have kindly offered to donate shingles and paint to repair the Netherfield and the bandstand. Our resident research team has volunteered their labor to help get everything ready."

One of the sculptors raised her hand. "We'd like to help, too, before we leave." She shot Marcus a dirty look. "We recognize an event like ours is at the mercy of the weather, and no one can tell an ocean what to do. We love Regency Bay, and we look forward to returning next summer."

"Thanks, Meg. You guys are part of our family and you're always welcome."

The police chief took the mic as Sophie stepped away. "Folks, if you're working on the cleanup, please come see me. Otherwise, I ask everyone to please clear the area." His steady gaze settled on Marcus in the crowd.

Sam tucked his camera into his gear bag and fell into step beside Sophie. "You okay? What happened?"

"A wicked squall blew through here around two a.m.—maybe you heard it."

He snorted. "I felt it. I had to get out of bed and shut my window. The glass was rattling in the frame for a while."

"Yeah. And when the sun came up, aside from the mess of tree branches and whatnot, a body washed up on the beach."

"I…uh…wow…I wasn't expecting that. You didn't have to see it, did you?"

She shook her head. "No. The first responders handled it."

He wrapped his arm around her shoulders, and she leaned into him for a moment before continuing on her way.

"It happens once or twice a year. Someone has too much to drink or takes a dare and thinks 'beach closed after sunset' doesn't apply to them. We do the best we can, but it doesn't matter how many signs we post—there's no way to isolate an entire beach."

"And Marcus and his buddies at Northanger will try to spin it to their favor?"

"Exactly." She caught his arm. "Look, please do me a favor? You don't have actual press credentials, so could you please stay clear of the police barricades?"

"Of course. I don't want to cause you any problems."

She smiled, though it was a bit pinched around the edges. "Thanks, really."

Chapter Seven

" 'Body washes up on beach. What does this say about our community?' " Wilf read in a monotone.

"We live next to an ocean and people who play stupid games win stupid prizes?" Bonnie muttered into her coffee cup.

Sophie ground the heels of her hands into her eye sockets. "What else?"

" 'Northanger Holdings' proposed construction would keep visitors safe.' "

Sophie raised her head. "From their own stupidity? How?"

"Funny you should ask. 'Our all-inclusive resort will feature an indoor saltwater wave pool, providing a safe place to enjoy the water even during inclement weather.' "

"Yeah, 'cuz no one ever drowned in a pool." *It's Monday morning and there is not enough caffeine in the world right now...* "The Chief said there was no indication of a crime. As soon as we receive the official report, we'll issue a statement—"

"With the statistics for accidental drowning deaths in oceans versus pools, as well as the standard admonishments to obey posted safety regulations?"

"Work our condolences to the victim's family in somewhere, would you?"

"Of course." He continued perusing the paper. "Oh.

Oh, dear…"

Sophie's head snapped up.

Bonnie scooted her chair over and grabbed the edge of the paper. " 'Mayor spotted carousing with visiting photojournalist.' "

"Carousing? What definition of carousing includes speaking with someone in extremely public venues?"

"Oh, it gets better," Bonnie continued, "Marcus also questions if your parents are getting insider information on town contracts. Because why else would they be so eager to help repair the damage from the storm?"

"Because they're good neighbors, maybe? They donated those supplies."

Wilf elbowed Bonnie aside and selected the next paper in the stack. "The Clarion: 'Community comes together to repair storm damage. Visiting sand sculptors offer aid to the town they love.' "

That's more like it.

"And in the style section, 'Cosplay group to hold annual costume ball. Will Mayor Bennet finally debut a new look?' "

Sophie glared at him. "It doesn't really say that."

Bonnie pushed in and read over his shoulder, then looked up with a shit-eating grin. "Yeah. It does."

****

By Thursday morning vendors were trickling in for the convention and setting up in their respective venues, including Sparrow, the costumer who'd offered Sophie the loan of a gown. Their elegant pastel gowns filled racks and display mannequins in the largest conference room at the Netherfield.

Sophie turned slowly in front of the mirror. The gown she modeled was a softer blue than her old one, with a filmy white lace overlay and a satin sash under the bust. And it didn't require a hoop or worse yet, a corset.

"You look amazing," Bonnie gushed. "Wait 'til the hottie sees you."

"Can you please not call him that?"

"But he is." She elbowed Sparrow. "Saturday night you can let me know what you think."

"Are you sure you want to loan this to me?" Sophie asked. *And do I have to sign a waiver stating I won't get within ten feet of a punch bowl while I'm wearing it?*

"Absolutely." Sparrow shoved a lock of pink ombre hair behind their ear. They were tall and lanky, with caramel-colored skin. Bike shorts and a T-shirt depicting two characters from a popular musical showcased their leanly muscled form. Sparkly red flipflops completed the ensemble. Their voice was low-pitched and soothing. "It'll be like when those big-time designers loaned gowns to the president's daughters for the state dinner. And if you want to keep it, I'll make you an excellent deal. It's stunning and it suits you perfectly."

Fresh start. No baggage. "And we're sure there's no impropriety?"

Bonnie snapped her gum, earning a horrified look from Sparrow, who grabbed a wastebasket and pointedly held it out.

Bonnie rolled her eyes, but deposited the wad of gum.

"Nope. Wilf checked. If the organization running the convention—the entity doing business directly with the town—offered you a gift beyond a certain material value, there could be a question, but this is an arrangement between a vendor and an individual."

"As a vendor, I set my own prices. It'd be

worthwhile to me knowing you're wearing one of my designs at future functions."

Bonnie stepped close beside Sophie, so they were both reflected in the mirror and draped an arm around her shoulders. "Soph, you bought the other dress years ago for a ball where you ended up getting dumped. It's time." She gave Sophie a playful little squeeze. "Sam's a good guy."

"And you know this how?"

Bonnie rolled her eyes. "Because he hangs around with my boyfriend. And also, because I ran a background check on him."

"I cannot believe you did that."

"Hey—we've been best friends since second grade. I want you to be happy."

Sophie blinked away a sudden sheen of tears.

Sparrow smirked and wrapped their arms around both Bonnie and Sophie. "Group hug!"

Someone cleared their throat cleared loudly and entirely too close and the three broke apart.

"So, this is how you spend the taxpayers' money, Mayor Bennet?"

Jeez, he's like a cockroach. Sophie turned slowly and faced the menace lurking in the corridor. "No, Marcus. I don't expense my clothing, I pay for it out of my own pocket."

"It still comes from the taxpayers."

"Yes, and your paycheck comes from your subscribers, but once it hits your bank account is it your money or theirs?"

"Mine, of course."

"And once my stipend is deposited in my account, it's my money and I can spend it as I see fit."

"On dress up clothes."

"Marcus, pretty much everyone who lives here owns or rents Regency clothing."

"Purchased from local vendors."

Sparrow set their hands on their hips and went toe to toe with Marcus. "If you must know, local shops sell my dresses and local brides order from me. You're blocking my display, so I'd appreciate it if you moved along."

****

Later that afternoon Sam tapped on Sophie's office door and grinned at the sign tacked into the wood:

No, I don't own the bookstore.

No, the school isn't named for my family.

Neither is the road.

Yes, I am aware Jane Austen didn't write a Sophie Bennet.

I'm a coincidence, not a character.

"You can have it when I'm finished, Wilf!" Sophie called through the closed door.

"Not Wilf, and I come bearing lunch. Or possibly dinner. Whichever you haven't eaten."

"Sam? Enter if you dare."

He pushed open the door with his elbow, juggling a takeout bag and cardboard drink caddy. "You have a reputation for skipping meals when you're busy." He glanced around curiously. Eight different colored plastic bins, each labeled for a particular weekend event and overflowing with relevant files, posters and boxes of fliers, stood in a row against the wall.

"Guilty." She moved whatever she'd been working on aside and made grabby hands.

He chuckled and passed her a cardboard clamshell box. "I have turkey sandwiches—no lettuce because you pick it off of everything, iced tea, and brownies."

"I think I'm in love."

Funny you should phrase it like that. He moved a box from the local printer off the guest chair and sat down.

She smooshed her sandwich and took a huge bite, following it up with a chomp of her pickle spear.

He took a more decorous bite of his own sandwich and wiped his mouth. "Seriously, when's the last time you ate?"

"I had a bagel this morning."

"It hasn't been morning for a few hours."

She shrugged. "I got busy."

"I have a present for you, but you need to eat your sandwich before I give it to you."

"Jeez, are you the big brother or something?" She took another healthy bite.

Ouch. He pushed away his food.

She lowered her sandwich. "Did I say something?"

He manufactured a smile. "No, it's not you. I am in fact, the younger brother. The one who insisted on pursuing a creative career instead of going off to business school or law school like a good little minion."

She reached across the desk for his hand. "Crap. I'm sorry. I didn't mean to—"

"Not your fault. There's no way you could have known." He squeezed her fingers. Her hand was smaller than his, but her grip was warm and firm. *Reliable, like her*. He winced. Reliable isn't a word too many women would appreciate. "Go on and eat your sandwich."

"I will if you will."

"Deal." He took a nibble of his food. "My older brother is the perfect son—corporate lawyer, married to a lawyer, first kid on the way—the whole shebang. I don't understand half the things he says in casual conversation. No way in hell could I have made it through years of statutes and contracts in a classroom. He's got some sort of regulatory job in Sacramento—making sure big companies follow all the rules."

"It sounds like important work."

"Our folks keep hoping I'll 'come around.' They drop all sorts of hints it's not too late and they'll cover the cost for business school, which is incredibly generous of them, but it's not what I want."

"But you're so talented. How can they ask you to give up a career you love?"

He took another bite, not tasting it at all. "They think photography is a lovely hobby, but not a suitable career."

"Finish your food so I can have my brownie—and my present."

"Yes, ma'am." He finished his sandwich while she plowed through her pickle and chips. "What about you? What does your family think of what you do?"

"Well, my folks are kinda laid back. They'd prefer it if Benjamin's stayed in the family, but they never give me a hard time about it. When the town started introducing all the environmental initiatives, they were the first business to comply—and then some."

"Yeah?"

"They went from running an old-school hardware store with bins of nails and screws to being the place that can special order anything. They stock lots of energy efficient and ecofriendly supplies, and my mom can find literally anything on the internet. The folks who own the rides on the amusement pier come to her to locate all sorts of vintage fittings and fixtures."

"Your folks sound amazing."

She grinned at him with an acquisitive sparkle in her brown eyes. "So…can I have my present now?"

He made a show of inspecting her empty lunch container. "Yep. Here's your prize for being a member of the clean plate club." He fished a tissue-wrapped rectangular parcel from his bag and passed it across the desk.

She tore off the paper and revealed a photo in one of the recycled plastic frames from Seaside Sundries. "Oh my God, I love it! Thank you." She set the framed shot of Octavia and her baby accompanied by a SCUBA-clad researcher giving a thumbs up on the corner of the desk where she could see it whenever she looked up from her work.

"You said it was your favorite."

She covered her mouth, snickering. "You gave me a picture of Finn. You know Bonnie will try to swipe it."

"Then wouldn't she have to arrest herself?"

Still laughing, she stood and walked around the desk, arms extended. He stood and enfolded her in a hug. She was warm and soft in his arms, but he could feel her underlying strength. So much passion and courage in such a lovely package.

"Really, thank you." She leaned up and kissed his cheek. "I love it."

Chapter Eight

Sam tugged at the white silk scarf-thing knotted around his throat, hoping for a bit more oxygen. How did people breathe with starched shirt collars up around their ears? And the less said about skin-tight breeches and white knee socks, the better.

Finn and Bonnie sauntered past, the former looking as uncomfortable as Sam felt, and the latter resplendent in a blinding shade of green satin.

Bonnie elbowed him. "Quit fidgeting. You guys look great."

An individual with startling pink hair and a matching high-waisted gown nodded. "This thing is just a fun costume party." They glanced down at the random dark shoes on Sam's feet. "Although if you plan on attending the reenactor's ball, you might consider proper shoes. They're particular about historically correct sartorial details. I'm Sparrow. They/them, if you please." They fished a business card from the little purse hanging at their wrist. "I don't carry shoes, but I have sources. Shoot me an email if you want to up your game."

"Thanks. I'm Sam Trowbridge. Er…he/him."

"Pleased to meet you, Sam."

He tucked the card into a pocket. "The costume shop didn't have my size, and this is the only pair I packed besides sneakers." He glanced around the lobby of the Longbourn. "Have any of you seen Sophie?"

Bonnie laid a hand on his arm. "She's just finishing up a call in her office. I did her hair and helped with her dress. She'll be here."

Sam scanned the crowd again. He didn't watch that show, but it was popular enough for him to recognize a dozen or so iterations of the leading lady's gown. The lobby was a riot of color. Some of the women wore soft, wispy pastel gowns, while others sported eye-achingly bright colors and patterns. Most of the men wore dark breeches and coats, but there was a sprinkling of scarlet military uniforms, as well as a few in full suits to match their lady's gowns.

Bonnie's fingers tightened on his arm, and she nodded toward the door, smirking. He turned…and promptly forgot how to breathe. Sophie stood framed in the entrance, chatting with an older woman dressed in dark purple satin and sporting an absurd feathered headpiece. Instead of her usual utilitarian braids, Sophie's beautiful red hair was swept up in a soft knot surrounded by a circlet of pale blue silk flowers. Her gown was blue with filmy white lace and looked far more refined than many of the garish creations around her.

Bonnie snickered.

He blinked and stepped forward, reaching for Sophie's hand. "You look…"

She raised one delicate eyebrow, and a dimple he'd never noticed before sprang to life.

He cleared his throat. "For someone who's not into all this, you wear it like you were born to it."

Her gaze flickered over his outfit, down to his stupid shoes and all the way back up to his face. A blush crept up his neck beneath the damned stiff collar.

"You're not so bad yourself."

He huffed out a laugh, then leaned in and kissed her cheek. "You look absolutely beautiful."

She slipped her arm through his. "We don't have to stay long—just a couple of dances."

He laid his hand over hers and squeezed gently "Whatever you like, but it seems a shame to be planning our escape before we're even inside the ballroom." She chewed her lip uncertainly, so he winked and added, "Besides, I borrowed DVDs from the library so I could learn the dances. Don't you wanna see if I've got the moves?"

She scrunched her eyes shut, trying to restrain the laughter bubbling up. "Okay Fred, let's see what you've got."

"You're on, Ginger."

The dance currently taking place resembled an upscale square dance, with two rows of participants facing each other. People turned in the wrong direction or reached for the wrong partner as often as not, but they laughed it off, clapping heartily when the music ended. The band leader announced a new dance, and Sophie towed him out to the dance floor.

A sprightly Irish tune filled the air, and couples bounced and clapped and hopped more or less in time to the music. Of course, it wasn't one of the ones on the DVDs he'd studied. He faced Sophie, which was fine as long as he could mirror her movements. But then she turned left, and he turned...not left...and ended up holding hands with a rather portly older lady. Dammit. Okay...left hand, two steps, right hand—also not Sophie. Out of the corner of his eye, he saw her to his right, lips pressed together as if she was repressing giggles. Fine. He "accidentally" stepped to the right, clutched her hand like a lifeline and concluded the promenade with her. Unlike the rather large gentleman in the mustard yellow velvet suit, he managed to not stomp on anyone's feet—or hem. The person in the pink gown materialized, producing safety pins and a miniature sewing kit from their purse to aid the unfortunate victim of said stomping.

The music ended to much applause—and much gasping for breath. Some of the men bowed to their partners. Sam started to emulate them, but Sophie's eyes were sparkling as she smiled at him so instead he leaned down and kissed her. She gasped against his mouth, and he froze. *Oh crap...did I overstep?*

Then she slid one small white-satin-gloved hand to the back of his neck and pressed her warm lips against his. Smart phones flashed in his peripheral vision. Another couple bumped into them, and he realized the music had changed to a waltz while they were lost in their own world. He slid one arm around her and took her other hand, holding it against his chest instead of extended in a proper waltz hold. Which was fine, seeing as they were more swaying than dancing.

He skimmed his hand up and down her back, feeling delicate lace and tiny satin-covered buttons beneath his fingertips. Sophie melted into him, resting her cheek on his chest. He tugged her a little closer and pressed his lips to the crown of her head. He chuckled softly and Sophie tilted her head back and looked at him.

"What?"

"I'm in the ecotourism capital of California, wearing a silly rented costume and dancing with a woman who looks like a fairy tale princess. This might just be the best night of my life."

"Mine, too."

The band leader announced a break for the musicians and set up a playlist of sappy love songs which seemed to hold special significance for many people in the crowd. An uncomfortable number of people were glancing their way and Sophie's cheeks flushed pink, though he couldn't tell if it was from exertion or the attention.

"Want to grab a drink? Maybe a little air?"

"Please."

****

They strolled through to the hotel dining room, where finger foods and dainty bite-sized desserts were arrayed on a satin and lace draped banquet table. Waiters served beverages from a second buffet. Sophie shrank away from a laughing couple carrying cups of bright red punch.

"What would you like?" Sam asked.

"Something I can't spill all over myself. This dress is borrowed."

He winked. "So's my suit." He guided her to one of the small round tables and held her chair. "Be right back."

She took the opportunity to open her phone and check her email.

"Hey—no work—you're at a party with the hottie," Bonnie snatched the phone from her hand and plopped into an empty chair.

Sophie grabbed for her phone, but Bonnie held it out of reach.

"Give me that."

"Nope. This is the longest I've ever seen you stay at one of these things. Besides, you look happy. I can't remember the last time you looked this sparkly. No work tonight."

Sparrow paused by their table. "She's right. You look amazing. I should just give you that dress."

"No!" Sophie winced. *OMG, the headlines if that got out.* "I mean, I love it. If I decide to keep it, I'm paying you a fair price."

Sparrow unfurled their fan with a flick of their wrist. "We'll see." They grabbed Bonnie's arm, tugging her away from the table.

Sam returned carrying two dainty stemmed glasses. "What did I miss?"

"An intervention of an intervention. I think."

The corner of his mouth ticked up in a small smile. "If you say so." He passed her a glass. "It's lemon lime soda. No color. "

"Good choice." She clinked her glass against his and took a sip. "How are you enjoying your first Regency-ish experience?"

"It's definitely not boring. And the company is excellent." He took a sip of his drink. "What about you? I've heard through the grapevine—"

"You mean Bonnie."

"Among others. They say you duck out of these things after one dance. How are you doing? We can go if you need to."

"I don't want to cut your first grand ball short."

He reached out and covered her hand with his own. "Hey, do I look like someone who spends a lot of time at balls? We can go whenever you're ready."

"Maybe another dance when the band comes back? And then maybe something a little less crowded?" Heat flared in her cheeks. *Oh my God, did I really say that?*

Out loud? It sounds like—

A mischievous twinkle in Sam's eyes suggested he knew exactly how her sentence could be misconstrued, but he chose not to. "A stroll on the boardwalk, maybe? I understand a lot of things stay open all night for this shindig, including the amusement pier."

She shuddered, visions of old gum and sticky ice cream spills dancing in her mind's eye. "I am not going on rides in a borrowed gown."

"Fair enough. But my clothes are in my car, and Bonnie mentioned you changed in your office, so...?"

"So, we could get changed, and I could check my email and borrow a pager since Bonnie absconded with my phone."

Sam chuckled. "Yeah, about your phone." He produced the missing item from his jacket pocket. "Finn had an idea being incommunicado would make you crazy, so he swiped it back."

"My heroes."

He stood and bowed, then offered her his arm like a scene from an old movie.

****

Sam was waiting when she emerged from town hall, back in her comfy—and washable—shorts and top. He was also his familiar twenty-first century self. He extended a hand, and she took it, twining her fingers with his. *This is real, at least for now. I can enjoy it for a few weeks.*

"Not to be wildly inappropriate, but how did you get out of that dress by yourself?"

She quirked an eyebrow.

His cheeks reddened. "I mean...all those little buttons?"

She chuckled and let him off the hook. "The buttons are for show. There's a hidden zipper. Sparrow is awesome about making their outfits comfortable."

"Right. So, where do you want to start?" He leaned in close, and his warm breath tickled her ear.

"Anywhere you like. The whole boardwalk is open all night. This is about as close as this town comes to Mardi Gras." She dodged aside as a group of Regency-clad revelers erupted out the door of the psychic shop comparing fortunes.

"Are you hungry? Since we're no longer concerned about ruining clothes that don't belong to us?"

She shook her head. "I can wait. Every place is crowded and it's a gorgeous night. Maybe whatever food carts catch our eye?"

"Okay, but someday I want to take you someplace nice for dinner." He steered them toward the sound of calliope music. "I know Bonnie's planning to party 'til dawn, so who's minding the boardwalk?"

She bumped her head against his shoulder. "The chief of police is on call tonight, and we brought in county police and private security to help."

They wove around stilt walkers, jugglers, and crowds of guests in more or less historical outfits. She clutched Sam's hand so they wouldn't be separated.

"This is incredible," he said, over the laughter, music, and snap of the sea breeze. "I've never seen anything like it."

"You don't have your camera. I don't think I've ever seen you without it." *For definitions of ever meaning "the last two weeks."*

He shrugged. "I'm not working tonight. I do however have my phone." He held it up and took a selfie of the two of them just as the Oliver and Octavia mascots strolled up and crowded into the frame. "Sometimes it's so easy to get caught up in capturing the moment, you forget to live in the moment." He brushed a kiss to her cheek. "And right now, I very much want to be present in this moment with you."

The amusement pier was as crowded as the brightest afternoon, although there were no kids in sight this late, and the ride operators were on the lookout for people who'd been overindulging. She could hardly blame them—no one wanted to spend the night hosing barf out of a ride vehicle. The scents of cotton candy, fried clams, and popcorn swirled around them, and her stomach rumbled.

Sam chuckled. "Ready to check out those food carts yet?"

She shook her head. "Rides first." She dragged him over to the triple decker carousel, a glittering confection of lights, mirrors, and a glorious menagerie of hand carved animals.

Sam followed her to the upper deck. "This is magnificent."

"It's over a hundred years old and it's been rebuilt a few times." She chose one of the elaborately carved benches and he settled beside her, draping his arm along the back of the seat. "I love the view from up here even better than the Ferris wheel."

"So do I," Sam murmured, although he stared at her, not the scenery.

A flush warmed her cheeks at his scrutiny. The ride began to move and the delicate updo Bonnie had created lost its battle with the breeze. *Dammit.* She scraped hair out of her mouth and tried to gather the rest back from her face.

"Don't." Sam grasped her wrists and gently pulled her hands away. He cupped her cheek in one hand and trailed the other through a lock of her hair. "You're so beautiful."

A half-formed protest went unsaid as he threaded his hand through her hair and pressed his lips to hers. They were softer than she expected, and she shifted closer until she was almost in his lap. She curled her hand into the soft cotton of his T-shirt, feeling the hammering of his heart. Or maybe hers. Both?

The ride slowed and Sam pulled back slowly, looking as breathless as she felt. He tucked her hair behind her ears with a slightly dazed smile.

Chapter Nine

Sophie was still smiling Monday morning when she arrived at town hall. Bonnie sat slumped at her desk, wearing sunglasses indoors with an oversized mug of coffee and a bottle of aspirin in front of her.

"Good morning," Wilf boomed.

Bonnie groaned.

"Did you sleep at all this weekend?"

Bonnie peeked over the top of her shades and smirked. "Wouldn't you like to know?"

"No, we would not," Wilf assured her. He passed Sophie her daily iced coffee beverage.

She kissed his cheek and curled into his guest chair before taking a long sip. "Okay. What's the damage?"

"Surprisingly little, considering the volume of guests the convention attracts. A half dozen drunk and disorderly and two DUIs, all controlled quickly without collateral damage. Perhaps next year we might consider setting up a shuttle service to and from the overflow hotels."

"Use the school buses?"

He nodded.

"Could you write me up a—"

He passed her a bullet-point list and attached cost analysis.

"Proposal." She grinned. "Thanks. What else?"

"Twenty-seven heat and sun related injuries, mostly

involving guests in costume. Three required transportation to the hospital for further treatment. The Clarion has full coverage of the winners of the costume contest and the ball. A lot of merchants are sold out of a variety of goods, mostly food and beverage, but they anticipated, based on past years, and placed orders ahead of time. Everything should be restocked in a day or so. Recycling containers are overflowing, but again, we scheduled an extra pickup, based on past years." He took a sip of his coffee, thumping the mug down on his desk.

Bonnie winced.

Sophie ignored her dramatics. "I think we need to give the go-ahead for the autumn murder mystery event."

Wilf nodded. "We can't accommodate any more traffic for this one."

"Can we do it?"

"I think so. We can use this event as a template. I believe the main competition would be fall renaissance faires or harvest events, rather than the screamy haunted house sort of thing. We should check with the hotels to see what their projected occupancy is. Levels drop after Labor Day."

"Extra cash before the holidays is always a good thing. Let's see if we can pull this together."

Wilf nodded and made more notes on his legal pad before continuing down his list. "The Norland is having plumbing issues, but Jake is on it, and they should be straightened out in plenty of time for next weekend."

"Everything's on track for the bird-watchers?"

Bonnie snorted into her coffee cup. "Birdies aren't near as popular as guys in tight breeches."

"Maybe, but it's revenue, and there's also a bunch of weddings next weekend." She took a deep breath.

"Okay, what did Marcus do this time?"

Wilf sighed and cleared his throat. " 'Debauchery and public indecency on the boardwalk. Is this the sort of town we want to raise our families in?' "

"Marcus doesn't have a family," Bonnie declared, "he crawled out from under a rock."

"Does he pull this stuff out of thin air? Public indecency? Most of the guests were in full costume with about a thousand percent more coverage than the average family on the beach." Sophie peered over the top of her cup. "And?"

" 'Mayor cavorts at ball in borrowed finery.' With a picture."

She grabbed the paper. Yup. It was indeed a picture of her and Sam, captured mid-kiss. She huffed irritably. "You know that kiss lasted a whole maybe five seconds." *Unlike the ones that came later*. "It's not as if Sam and I were—and how did he even get this? I didn't see him skulking around."

Bonnie waved her phone. "It was perfect romantic moment in the middle of a grand ball. There were tons of pictures. Didn't you notice all the flashes? Anyone could have slipped it to him for a few bucks."

"He might even have grabbed it from social media," Wilf added.

"Fine. Whatever. It's done." She straightened in her seat. "Bird-watching?"

"Bird-watching," Wilf agreed, reaching for an overstuffed file folder.

****

"Bird-watching?" Sam asked curiously.

"Yup."

He eyed a smirking gull strutting down the center of

the boardwalk.

She elbowed him. "Those aren't the only kind of sea bird, you know. Besides, this event draws a different crowd. The research pier gets attention and a lot of the folks who were run ragged this past weekend get a little break. It's not as busy, so the hotels can book weddings."

"So romance is dead? At least for next weekend?"

"The romance writers descend on us the following weekend." She huffed out a breath of laughter. "Anyway, plenty of people find the sea romantic. There's a sunrise boat cruise you might want to check out. People get amazing pictures."

Water and early morning light…challenging, but could definitely be worth it. If… "I'll go if you will."

"I—" Her phone chirped an alarm. "—I've got a tour in fifteen."

A family ambled past, sharing a funnel cake in all its messy glory. *Which reminds me…* "When's the last time you ate?"

"Um…" A guilty flush crept up her cheeks.

He dug a chocolate chip cereal bar from the depths of his bag and held it out.

"I can grab a corn dog or something."

He rolled his eyes. "Or you can pass out in the middle of a tour. Take it."

Her fingers brushed his as she took the foil wrapped treat. "Thanks."

"How about we discuss the boat ride over dinner tonight?"

"I have three tours—"

"Tell me what time you're done. I'll meet you here and we'll go to the Anchor. Food. Containing actual protein."

****

The outdoor deck at the Anchor wrapped around three sides of the weathered building. Sam chose a table facing toward town, instead of out to sea. A row of local shops faced the pub, and the streets beyond were filled with skinny wooden houses rather more faded and working class than their grand cousins in San Francisco. *Is one of them hers?*

The breeze spun the yellow beer-logoed umbrella shading their table from the last glare of sunset. Sam could barely hear the occasional woofs of local canines roughhousing in nearby Dogsfield Park—the pooch haven was his new favorite spot in town. He glanced at Sophie's plate—she'd demolished about half their shared basket of Daisy's famous fish and chips. "You might consider eating more than one meal a day."

She shrugged and patted her mouth with a napkin. "I forget when I'm busy."

"When's the last time you weren't busy?"

"Probably not since before I was elected."

He scooped a few more fries onto his plate then speared another forkful of flakey white fish.

"When will you know? About your movie, I mean?"

He chewed and swallowed. "I'm not sure. I'm contracted through Labor Day. I keep taking pictures and sending them in every Friday." He glanced around the cozy street. "I hope it works out in a way that's good for the town. I really like it here."

"If they go ahead and make the movie, what then? Would there be something for you to do?" She looked down at her plate, then back up at him. "I mean, could you stay here in town?"

Does she want me here as much as I want to stay?

And how can I convince her she can trust me with her heart? He set down his fork and steepled his hands. "I don't know. I've never worked on a project like this before. I would think there'd be something for a still photographer to do. Would you want me to?"

"Very much."

He reached across the table and took one of her hands. "I can't say what the future will bring, but this, right now? Spending time with you? I'm liking this a lot."

Her lips curled in a smile. "Me, too."

He lifted her hand to his lips and kissed it.

"Are you going native on me?" she teased.

"Maybe." He released her hand and returned his attention to his dinner. "What time is the cruise?"

"Sunrise is six, so the boat boards at five."

He winced. "So, we need to be there at four thirty?"

A smirk hovered around the corners of her mouth. "Yup. Sure you want to go?"

"If it means we can spend the day together, yes."

"Okay then. I guess I'll see you Saturday morning."

"No!" She stared at him, and a flush crept up his neck. "I mean…it's just…Saturday's a long way off. Jeez, I sound like a horny teenager."

Sophie's shoulders relaxed and her cheeks blushed a delicate rose.

"What about the Wednesday Night Beach Movie?"

One side of her mouth ticked up in a little half smile. "Seriously? You want to sit on a beach in the dark and watch a shark eat beach goers?"

"Maybe I want to sit on the beach in the dark and cuddle with a gorgeous woman."

She bit her bottom lip, then dug in her bag for her

phone. "Here." She passed it across the table. "Add yourself to my contacts and I'll text you, so you have my number."

He took the phone and started typing. "To set up a meeting time for the movie?"

"Or…in case two days is too long to wait."

It definitely is.

****

Sam tightened his arms around Sophie, watching images flicker on the movie screen. "That dude gives small town mayors a bad name," he murmured in her ear. She shifted closer, almost into his lap. Their legs tangled together beneath an oversized beach towel. Not that he minded. *Blessings for sand chairs without arms.*

"He really does."

The crowd on the beach gasped in feigned horror as the familiar music swelled and the on-screen ocean turned red. Many took the darkness, stiff sea breeze, and on-screen mayhem for a good excuse to snuggle with their companions. Bonnie and another deputy patrolled with flashlights, a silent reminder to keep things from becoming too amorous. Their presence was a strong incentive to keep his hands in plain sight…although he was grateful for his jacket and Sophie's sweatshirt adding a layer of protection from temptation.

"Has this sort of thing ever happened here?"

She twisted in his embrace. "A bad mayor? In *my* town?"

He chuckled, rubbing his hands up and down her arms. "No. A shark."

"Contrary to what Hollywood would have you believe, shark attacks in California are very rare. Much less common than accidental drownings. Plus, some of us actually listen when the Coast Guard issues warnings. Why? Having second thoughts about the boat ride?"

He pressed his lips to the crown of her head. "Nope. Well, not really. It's just…"

"What?"

"It's a big shark and *lot* of teeth."

"It's a fake shark on a movie screen."

"Yeah, I know but I've only ever seen it on TV before." He winced at the on-screen action.

"Stan—the harbormaster—is super diligent about his job. The boat won't go out if there's the slightest danger." She smirked gleefully. "But if you're scared, I'll hold your hand."

"I'd like that."

Chapter Ten

Sophie's flip flops pattered against the timbers of the boardwalk. Usually there was too much ambient noise to notice, but even the gentle lap of the surf seemed loud in the predawn hush. Flags and pennants flapped listlessly in the early morning breeze. *I should do this more often.* The dim overnight lights in the bookstore window showcased a display of nature and conservation titles. One of the boardwalk kitties trotted past with something clenched in its jaws she was just as happy not to see clearly.

The savory scent of frying bacon drifted from the diner and her stomach growled. She ignored it, settling her bag on her shoulder and heading for the research pier. Lady Catherine's was open as well. A line outside their takeout window snaked down the boardwalk and people toting camera bags and binocular cases clustered around the coffee carts.

" 'Morning, Sophie!" the delivery man from the Clarion called as he dropped a bundle of papers in front of Seaside Sundries.

She waved. A cardboard cup that somehow escaped the litter patrol skittered along the boardwalk. She stooped and picked it up, depositing it in the proper bin.

"Never off duty, are you?"

Sophie whirled. "Jeez, give me a heart attack, why don't you?"

"Hey, we have a date, remember?" Sam offered one of the coffee cups he carried.

"I…yeah, we do." She chewed her lip before reaching for the cup. "Thanks."

"So why so surprised to see me?"

"Bonnie may have mentioned she saw you heading out of town last night." She took a sip, steam curling around her face in the early morning coolness.

"I had an errand to run, that's all." He bumped her arm gently. "I am not that guy, okay? Even if something happened and I couldn't make it today, I would have called. I'd never just disappear on you."

She sucked in a deep breath. "You're right. Sorry. I did warn you I might get a little weirded out occasionally."

"Hey—it's okay." He winked. "You're worth a little weird."

She snickered.

"Or something. That sounded better in my head." He held out his free hand and Sophie took it, twining their fingers together as they strolled toward the lights of the research pier. "It's so odd for all the bustle to be over this way while the amusement pier is dark and quiet."

"Don't worry—everything'll be business as usual by the time the boat gets back."

They turned onto the research pier. The Oliver and Octavia mascots gamboled in front of the lit up entrance of the visitors' center. He sported a blue bow tie and brandished a toy camera with a large, old-fashioned flash bulb. She wore a blue hair bow and a pair of binoculars on a strap around her neck.

"How many outfits do they have?"

"More than I do," Sophie chuckled. She pulled up a

receipt on her phone and passed it to the attendant at the ticket window. "Good morning. Two for the sunrise cruise under the name Bennet."

Sam looked up from his phone. "I thought I had this one?" He showed her his receipt for two tickets.

"I thought I did?"

The kid at the counter, who looked like he was in dire need of more caffeine, shrugged. "I can refund one of you. Or one ticket for each. Whatever you prefer."

"I've got it," Sophie said.

The kid shrugged again and passed her two wrist bands, then handed two more to Sam. He turned to the next people in line behind them, a pair of college-age girls clutching notebooks and field guides.

"Have you guys purchased your tickets already?"

They looked at the kid at the desk, who was much more observant when addressing two pretty girls his own age. "It's legit," he assured them. "He and his date forgot whose turn it was."

Sophie's cheeks heated hearing the word "date" announced so casually, but no one else seemed to notice.

One of the girls smiled at Sam. "Thanks. We can pay you—"

"It's fine. Enjoy your day." He handed them the wristbands, then offered Sophie his arm. "See? Chivalry isn't dead after all. Even on bird-watchers' weekend."

"It was nice of you to give them your tickets." She leaned up on her toes and kissed his cheek.

"Well, I've never met a college student who didn't welcome more cash for snacks. Speaking of which—"

She laughed and squeezed his arm. "I thought we'd hit the bakery after the cruise. They make the most amazing chocolate croissants."

"Funny how you remember to eat when there's chocolate involved."

"You say that like it's a bad thing."

"I think the kid at the ticket window is the first person I've encountered who doesn't know you're the mayor."

"To be honest, I'm not sure I'd have recognized the mayor at his age."

"I find that hard to believe."

The entrance opened into a gallery lit with shifting blue and green light. Tanks filled with a sampling of local underwater life lined the walls. Photos and infographics highlighted Oliver and Octavia and their growing family.

"This is stunning. I feel like I'm swimming underwater in the middle of the kelp forest."

"That's the idea." Sophie trailed her hand along the edge of the tidal pool touch tank. "I wish we could do one of those underwater galleries that looks out on the real thing."

"What's stopping you?"

"Funds, for one thing. There would also need to be a ton of studies about the impact of the construction—"

"And the increased number of visitors?"

"Mm-hm."

A cacophony of barks echoing from the rehab pool in the next gallery cut off further conversation.

" 'Morning, Finn," Sam called over the racket.

Finn looked up and waved with a fish in each hand. He tossed them in the water to the delight of the pool's occupants.

"How many do you have in there?" Sophie asked.

"Two."

They crossed the painted red line into the splash zone around the pool where two juvenile harbor seal pups frolicked, one with healing gashes on its back.

"These two little things are making all that noise?" Sam asked, reaching for his camera.

"They can be heard as far as a kilometer away, so's their mama can find them if they're lost," Finn replied.

"But these two don't have moms?"

"We think the little one was snatched." Finn tossed a couple more fish.

"Snatched?"

Sophie pointed to the infographics surrounding the pool. Most were dedicated to the topic of not harassing local marine wildlife. "A lot of times, a mom leaves her baby while she goes for food. Well-meaning people see the pup and assume it's been abandoned. Mom surfaces, sees people and spooks."

Sam snapped a few quick shots. "So, they live here now?"

Finn grabbed his empty bucket. "Nah. There's not enough room here. Once they're stable, they'll be transferred to a bigger facility, then returned to the wild where they belong. You two going out on the boat?"

"We are."

Finn threw back his head and laughed. "We'll never get you aboard Queenie again."

"Huh?"

Sophie rolled her eyes. "History joke. The Prince George is the public tour boat. It has showier amenities for passengers. The Queen Caroline is the research boat. It's—"

"Not much to look at, but it gets the job done," Finn finished the sentence.

"I still don't get it. The boats look the same."

Sophie shook her head. "They're pretty much the same boat. They're state of the art, minimal emission vessels. The Queen Caroline is the more expensive of the two—it's just that the money went into labs, equipment, and holding pens, with basic accommodations for people."

"Very basic," Finn quipped.

"Hey, money doesn't grow on trees. You got the new underwater camera equipment you guys asked for."

"We sure did. Enjoy your bird-watching."

"Thanks. We will." Sophie towed Sam away from the rehab display.

The next gallery showed a film on the reclamation of Regency Bay, and a display of art created from recycled trash collected from the beach and bay clean up.

Sam paused in front of a picture of Sophie standing next to a truckload of garbage collected from the beach. "It's an extraordinary thing you've done."

She ducked her head, cheeks blazing. "It was a group effort. The whole town's been part of the reclamation program."

"But it started from an idea, and someone passionate enough to convince a group to come together and get their hands dirty collecting trash, then commit to a future of recycling, reusing, and not littering." He tucked a finger under her chin, tilting her face up. "That's you, Sophie." He leaned down and kissed her. His lips were warm and tasted faintly of the vanilla syrup he liked in his coffee.

****

Sam's senses reeled from the brief kiss. Sophie's hand wrapped around his own as they boarded the boat and found a good spot at the railing. She looked the most casual he'd ever seen her, in cutoffs over a blue bikini, with a faded plaid button down top to keep the sun off her shoulders. Although her clothes were quite modest by beach standards, there was enough soft, freckled skin on display he wished they were somewhere more private. Much more private.

She waited quietly beside him, leaning against the rail, while he adjusted his equipment to accommodate the low light. Her warm presence was soothing, and she didn't feel the need to chatter all the time. *Huh. Someday I'll have to hear the story of how she and Bonnie became such good friends.*

To the east, the sky lightened to a deep royal blue. Ever so slowly, streaks of cotton-candy clouds stained the sky—fuchsia and magenta, deepening into lavender and plum. He heard Sophie's breath catch in her throat.

"Can you really capture all these colors on film?"

"I can sure as hell try."

She didn't touch him while he worked, which he appreciated professionally. Personally, every nerve in his body sang with awareness of her proximity.

The bottom edge of the cloud bank blazed into orange, lighting the sky. The clouds drifted apart, and the fledgling sun was reflected in all its golden glory on the water. A flight of gulls decided it was indeed morning and launched themselves into the air, squawking raucously.

Sam finally lowered his camera.

Sophie wrapped her hands around his arm. "Was that worth crawling out of bed for?"

He leaned down and kissed the end of her nose. "Yes." He turned and slid his arms around her waist, tugging her close. "The sunrise was exquisite, but I believe I was promised birds that aren't gulls."

She twined her arms around his neck. "Sorry. I'm the mayor of the town, not the actual bay. If you don't like the selection of birds, you'll have to take it up with Mother Nature."

He leaned down and kissed her, then flinched as cold seawater spattered their faces. A small hawk shot up from the water with a wriggling, silvery-scaled fish clamped in its powerful beak.

"Or not," Sam muttered, looking at the sky in wonder.

Chapter Eleven

Sophie laughed as Sam dodged away from her hand. "Hold still! Your nose is turning red."

"Is this stuff gonna make me smell pretty?"

"No. It's reef-safe. No unnecessary chemicals."

He stopped dodging and let her dab sunscreen on his face. "Okay, but only if you allow me to return the favor."

"Deal." She passed him the tube of lotion and closed her eyes. His fingers glided delicately over her forehead, cheeks, and chin. She cracked one eye open. "You wouldn't want us to show up at the ball next week with peeling noses, would you?"

"Another ball?" He capped the sunscreen and passed it back to her.

She nodded, stuffing it into her bag. "Mm-hm. This one's for the Regency romance writers' thing. They decided to go costume optional this year."

He waggled his eyebrows and wrapped his arms around her. "Did they, now?"

She swatted him lightly in the chest. "Not like that! The dress code is Regency costume or black tie."

"I didn't pack a tux for a summer at the beach."

"You still have the costume you rented for last week? I mean, you don't have to—I can make a solo appearance and bow out after a dance or two—"

"And miss out on a chance to dance with the most

gorgeous woman in town again? Not happening." He hummed something off-key under his breath, swaying them to the tune—or lack thereof.

Sophie leaned in closer, ignoring the rush of bird-watchers to the other side of the deck to see a long-billed something or other. Sam tucked those pesky loose strands of hair behind her ear. His breath was warm against her face, scented with coffee and vanilla and—

Something splashed in the water beside them. Startled, they broke apart and saw a dolphin slapping the water with its tail flukes. The dolphin chittered at them, then dove beneath the waves.

"That was incredible!"

Sophie glanced around. "And I think we're the only ones who saw it."

Sam rested his forehead against hers. "So…chocolate croissants? Then what? What's next on the list of Sophie's favorite things?"

"Ordinarily, I'd say the nature preserve. It's usually less crowded than the public beach. But this weekend there's a bunch of guided tours for the bird-watchers." She chewed her lip. He'd either love this idea or hate it. "Do you have opinions on mini golf?"

"I don't think I've played since I was a kid. Did it even exist in Regency times?"

She rolled her eyes. "Probably not but…oh, hell, you sort of have to see this place to understand."

He kissed her forehead. "If you wanna show it to me, then I wanna see it."

****

He wasn't quite sure what he'd been expecting, but Regency Gardens was certainly a novelty. Lush beds of shrubs and summer flowers sheltered intricately detailed small-scale buildings. A flicker of motion caught his eye, and a garden-scale toy train chugged into view. True to Regency Bay form, a small sign assured visitors both gray water and drip irrigation systems were in place.

An English country village, London, and Regency Bay landmarks were replicated in miniature golf courses. Indoors, an upscale snack bar served exotic blends of iced tea, fresh lemonade, and petit fours. It should have been kitschy, but somehow it fit right in with the rest of the town.

"This is—"

Sophie squeezed his hand. "I know it's kinda goofy, but I've always loved coming here, since I was a kid."

"The buildings are incredible."

"At Christmas, they add tiny decorations and lights. It's a local tradition. They serve hot chocolate with real whipped cream and the most amazing peppermint brownies."

"I'd love to experience Christmas here." *With you.* Her beautiful brown eyes looked suspiciously shiny, so he slung an arm around her shoulders and gave her a little squeeze. "Is this one of the places the new development would displace?"

She nodded.

He pressed his lips to the crown of her head. "Then we'll have to make sure it doesn't happen."

She tilted her head and looked up at him. "We?"

"We. If it's important to you, it's important to me." He shifted, tightening his arms around her. "Look, I know I've only been here a few weeks, but I love this place. I'm going to help you fight for it."

"You really mean it?"

"I do."

"Hey, that's my line!" a woman in a plastic tiara and white satin "Bride" sash called as she and a giggling group of friends sauntered past on their way to the London course.

Sophie's face crinkled with laughter. "This place is also popular with bachelorette parties."

He shrugged. "I can think of worse things. So, we gonna play some mini golf?"

"I like the little village best."

"Sounds good to me. Can I put my arms around you to help you putt?"

She quirked an eyebrow. "What makes you think I need help?"

"Maybe I just want to put my arms around you."

****

Discovering the secret of the mini English village golf course was delightful—especially since they used kisses to keep score. And so much sun resulted in a scamper through the splash pad, laughing like little kids as they flicked water at each other.

Water dripped in his eyes as they squelched back to Sophie's truck, grinning like idiots.

She grabbed a couple of towels from a bag in the back and tossed one to him.

He mopped his face, trying not to stare at the way her damp clothes clung to her curves. "What's next on the agenda?"

"I'm thinking food?" She shoved a couple strands of loose hair behind her ears. "Have you been to Belle's yet?"

"No, but I've heard the food is amazing."

"Belle's it is." She stuffed her towel in the mesh bag in the back and hopped up into the driver's seat, hissing as her legs connected with the heat of the vinyl seat.

He followed suit, resting one hand on her knee and tracing idle patterns on her skin as she drove through the local streets. "This has been an amazing day."

She flashed him a grin before returning her attention to the road. "It has." She found a space on the street near the barbeque joint.

The scents of woodsmoke and sizzling beef made his mouth water as soon as he climbed out of the truck. Diners crowded the outside patio and waitstaff carrying heavy trays hustled between tables. Dozens of conversations buzzed over the merry songs of a visiting pirate band. "It smells incredible, but…"

She stopped and looked at him. "But?"

"Is it always this crowded?"

"Pretty much. We could grab takeout if you like. I don't have much of anything in my fridge."

"Why am I not surprised?" *But where would we go? I don't want to take her to the boarding house and have everyone knowing our business…*

She stood on the hot pavement, chewing her lip. "Would you like to get dinner to go and take it back to my place?"

"I'd like that very much, but only if you're comfortable."

"I'm a grown person and it's my home. I'm allowed to have company."

"As long as you're sure. I don't want to make waves for you."

****

As he'd suspected, Sophie's neighborhood was one of the streets of skinny clapboard houses. Most were pastel shades, trimmed in white or another modest color.

A solitary house stood out from its peach and lemon neighbors with a bold rainbow paint job, each architectural detail picked out in a different color.

"That must be murder to maintain."

"It's a labor of love, I assure you. It's in perfect condition, so no one can complain about it. This is me." She pulled into the driveway of a sky-blue house with white trim.

The now-familiar assortment of Regency Bay recycling bins lined the side of the house. Six steps led to the covered front porch. A wooden rocker painted a glossy royal blue stood to one side of the door and a pair of ginger and white cats snoozed inside on the windowsill.

Sam hopped out of the truck, juggling his bag and the fragrant shopping bag full of dinner. "Is this where the wet towels go?" He jerked his chin toward a folding drying rack on the porch.

Sophie slid down from the driver's side. "Yes, please." She grabbed her bag and the laundry bag from the back of the truck. "Here—let's swap."

He took the opportunity to kiss the end of her nose. "Don't get into those shrimp skewers without me."

"No promises! I told you—Belle's is the best."

Hearing voices—or more likely, smelling food, the two cats sat up and patted the window screen.

"Who are they?" Sam asked, shaking out the towels.

Sophie grinned, grabbing the mail from the box and stuffing it in the top of her bag. "This is Carb on the left and Ginny on the right."

He raised an eyebrow.

"Carburetor and Engine. And if you think that's bad, their siblings are Headlight, Tailpipe, and Muffler."

"Am I sensing a theme?"

"You're sensing my mechanic found them outside his shop one morning." She unlocked the front door and stepped inside. She turned into the open living room, dropped her bag on a chair and stepped out of her flipflops. "The door in the hallway is a powder room and you can leave your bag here if you want. There's a charging station on my desk if you need to plug anything in."

He toed off his soaked tennis shoes and followed her down a narrow hallway tiled in butter yellow linoleum to a small kitchen. The walls were painted soft yellow, making the room feel larger than it actually was, and the worn vinyl felt cool and smooth against his bare feet.

Sophie set their dinner bag on a table surrounded by four mismatched wooden chairs all painted the same sky blue as the cabinets. An eclectic selection of blue glassware and blue, white, and yellow dishes were displayed in a glass-fronted cupboard.

"How can I help?"

Two ginger and white streaks swarmed past, aiming for the table. Sophie caught one and gave her a snuggle and kiss before depositing her on the floor. "Could you guard our dinner while I feed these two?" She reached for a cabinet door with a cat tucked under her arm and the other twining around her ankles.

"Sure. Or I could set the table?"

She flashed him a grateful smile. "That would be great, thanks."

He opened the cupboard curiously, his gaze wandering over the harmonious selection of colors and shapes. "Is there two of anything in here?"

"I doubt it. I like to rummage around vintage shops

and antique fairs and pick whatever catches my eye."

Antiques, huh? Sounds like fun... "I love it." He took his time, choosing two blue, yellow, and white patterned dinner plates from different sets, a chunky pale blue highball glass, and a delicate royal blue stemmed goblet.

Sophie washed her hands at the sink and dried them on a cheerful blue and yellow plaid towel. She hesitated a heartbeat, then shrugged off her damp button down and hung it on a peg by the backdoor.

His breath stuttered in his throat. Granted, her bikini top was the sort designed to stay put during outdoor activity, but it showed a lot of delicate, freckled skin his hands itched to touch. Giving in to temptation, he stepped behind her and slipped his arms around her waist.

She flinched away from his damp shirt.

"Sorry." He leaned back and clawed the blue T-shirt over his head, then draped it over the back of one of the chairs. "Better?"

She nodded, leaning into him for a moment before opening the silverware drawer.

"I've got a dry shirt in my bag if you want me to—"

She glanced over her shoulder with a saucy little wink. "No...you're fine."

He kissed her cheek, then helped her transfer steaks and shrimp skewers to the waiting plates. "This smells incredible."

"Wait 'til you taste it." She squeezed a wedge of lime over the food, then turned and held out one of the skewers.

He nibbled a bit of shrimp off awkwardly, trying not to get poked by the business end of the skewer. It was worth the effort, as the tangy grilled seafood flavor exploded across his tongue.

"You're gonna put your eye out." She slid the remaining bit of shrimp off the stick and fed it to him, then helped herself to another.

"Hey—whose shrimps are those?"

"Whoever gets to them first." She ducked under his arm carrying both plates.

Ooohhh…is that how it's gonna be? Game on. He grinned and followed her to the table.

Chapter Twelve

After dinner, they cleaned up, weaving in and out of each other's space with the sort of easy familiarity unexpected for such a brief acquaintance. Ginny wound around Sam's ankles and Sophie nudged her with her toes.

"Stop it. You've been fed and cats don't get people food."

Sam flushed an adorable shade of scarlet, and she chose not to mention how many times she'd seen his hand dip under the table during dinner. He hung up the dish towel and smoothed it on the oven door handle. "I guess I should be going."

Sophie glanced at him, catching her lip between her teeth. "You don't have to. I mean…I'd like it if you stayed."

He tucked a finger under her chin, tipping her face up. "I'd like that, too."

Her cheeks warmed. "Would you like another drink? I think there's a bottle of wine around here somewhere."

"It's been a long day, and I'd like to keep a clear head. Water's fine."

He's probably right. "How about fizzy water?"

She grabbed a green glass bottle from the fridge, and he selected two more mismatched glasses from the cabinet. They moved to the living room and settled on her couch with the comfy-soft blue slip covers.

Best investment I ever made. The center section was as long as a standard couch, and the two corners had matching ottomans. The whole thing formed a cozy u-shape, perfect for binging movies—not that she could recall the last time she'd done such a thing—or snoozing with a book. Or…

A wooden tray on one of the ottomans served in lieu of a coffee table. Sam set down their glasses and sat, draping his arm across the back of the sofa. She felt the weight of his gaze while she puttered around, turning off the hall light and pulling the drapes shut.

Sophie unclipped her hair and her braid tumbled down over her shoulder. She tossed the clips and hair tie in her bag and grabbed a brush. Then she crossed to the couch and sat, curling one leg underneath herself.

"Here—let me," he offered.

She shifted around, and he undid her braid. She shivered deliciously when he ghosted a kiss to the back of her neck.

"Can I ask you something?" He separated sections of her hair with careful fingers, never tugging.

"Sure."

"You told me about the jerk who jilted you in college, but…you haven't been alone since then, have you?" He held out a hand for her brush.

She huffed out a breath of laughter. "No, I haven't been walled up in a tower all these years. Or shipped off to Coventry. I've dated here and there. I just…don't do casual very well." A contented little sound escaped her throat as he pulled the brush through her hair. "And…one time I followed Bonnie's advice. There was a summer researcher…"

"You don't have to—"

"No, it's fine. He made it very clear from the beginning he was going back east at the end of the summer, so I wasn't heart broken or anything, but…" She shook her head, despite his fingers tangled in her hair. "I don't know how Bonnie does it. I just—"

He laid a steadying hand on her shoulder and finished brushing her hair. "You don't do casual." He tossed the brush on the tray and ran his fingers through her hair.

She wriggled around on the couch until she faced him again, tucking her legs up on the seat.

"Look, I can't promise you forever, not tonight. But I have no urgent plans to depart for the far side of the country after Labor Day. I'm looking for fall gigs in this area."

"So you can stay?"

"So I can stay." He took her hand, rubbing his thumb over her knuckles. "And whatever happens, I promise we'll talk about it. I won't just disappear. Okay?"

She sucked in a deep breath to calm her racing heart. *This isn't a fairy tale. It's real life. He's being honest. I can't ask anything more.* "Okay."

He tenderly tucked a lock of hair behind her ear. "You're so beautiful."

"I've been out in the sun and wind all day—"

He laid a finger on her lips. "You're beautiful."

She glanced at him through her lashes. His intent green-eyed gaze and all his attention were focused on her. His contemplation was a palpable thing, and a flush crept up her cheeks.

"What was your mysterious errand last night? Bonnie thought maybe you were trying to skip town."

"I know she's your best friend, but sometimes Bonnie needs to mind her own business." He rubbed the back of his neck. "I had to make a purchase."

"And you couldn't buy whatever it was here in town?"

"I could, but—oh, hell." He fished a small package from his back pocket.

Her eyes widened. "Oh."

He raked a hand through his hair. "I wanted to be prepared...just in case...I mean if we decided...if you wanted...but I didn't want to buy them in town and have people saying things about us...you..."

"You're kind of adorable when you're not forming complete sentences."

"Not sure adorable is what I was going for."

She shifted closer and draped her arms around his neck. "It works." She pressed a kiss against the side of his neck, inhaling his warmth, flavored with a hint of salt and sunscreen.

He cradled her in his arms. "We don't have to do anything you don't want."

"I want this." She ran her hands over his chest.

His heartbeat pounded beneath her fingers and his green eyes focused on hers as he stroked her cheek. "You tell me what you like, okay? Or what you don't like. I want this to be good for you."

"I'm not sure? It's been a while." She glanced down, then back up through her lashes. "And it goes both ways, you know."

"It's okay. We can figure it out together." He traced one of her bikini straps with his fingertips, tickling along the swell of her breast and leaving a delicious trail of goose bumps in his wake.

"Okay." She darted in and pressed her lips to his before she lost her nerve. His shoulders were tense beneath her hands, so she shifted her grip, massaging the rigid muscles until they relaxed under her touch.

Sam's hands wandered, mapping her rib cage and the lines of her bikini top. He skimmed a hand up her back and fingered the clasp. "Is this okay?" he murmured against her mouth. She nodded and he undid the catch. She gasped as the straps loosened, but she helped him guide the top off and drop it…somewhere. She raised one arm across her breasts instinctively, then lowered it, chewing her lip.

Sam cupped her face in his hands and gently dislodged her lip from between her teeth, then kissed her deeply. One hand slipped from her cheek and touched the newly revealed flesh, stroking and caressing her with careful fingers. She arched into his touch with a breathy little moan. Encouraged, he flexed his fingers and dragged his thumb across her nipple.

She shifted into his lap, and Sam responded, supporting her with a hand against her back. His other hand drifted to her thigh, stroking from her knee up to the hem of her shorts, then under the edge of the material.

He trailed hot kisses down her throat, and she slid her hands into his hair, combing through the thick ebony locks, soft and warm as the fur of some exotic cat. This close to him, his…interest…was obvious. She slid her palm down his chest, dancing over firm abs to the button of his shorts.

He froze. "Are you sure?" he murmured against her skin.

"Very."

He dropped his hands to her waist and unfastened

her shorts. She lifted her hips and helped him slide them down her legs and off, leaving her in just the blue bikini bottom. He shifted them to lay back on the sofa and Sophie pushed up on her elbows, feeling the weight of his gaze. He leaned over her, keeping his weight propped up off of her while his hand wandered. He kneaded her breast, then trailed his hand down to the edge of the bikini bottom, tugging at the elastic band. She nodded and he slid his hand inside. His hands and lips were so warm and gentle, touching places no one had since— *nope. Not gonna think about anyone else but him. Just Sam.*

She surged up and kissed him, letting her own hands explore. Her fingers mapped a thin, raised scar along his ribcage.

He flinched slightly. "That tickles."

"Sorry." She traced it with her fingertips. "How'd you get it?"

"Souvenir of my wreck diving certification. Wrecks include fun accessories like rusty old nails."

"I didn't know you were certified."

"Can't get interesting photos unless you go interesting places."

"I can think of a few interesting places we could go."

"Funny. I was thinking the same thing." He grinned and moved his mouth to a *very* interesting spot at the hinge of her jaw.

She stroked the front of his shorts, then popped the button and worked the zipper down. He stood and let his clothes slide to the floor, then bent and retrieved one of the condoms from the package.

"Still okay?"

She nodded again, bottom lip caught between her

teeth, as he slipped her bikini bottom off. His hands lingered on her waist, moving her to recline against a pile of throw pillows. He dipped a hand between her legs, stroking and exploring with gentle fingers. He curled his finger in just the right spot and pleasure buzzed through her body.

"Good?"

She nodded and adjusted her legs as he loomed over her, mindful of his weight even as he slid home. A tiny gasp escaped her mouth as she grew accustomed to the feel of him. *I don't remember this feeling as good the last time. It's like he's a piece of my life I didn't even know was missing.*

He brought one hand up and cupped her cheek as he began to move.

She turned her head and kissed his palm, then focused her gaze on his gorgeous sea-glass-green eyes. Her breath quickened at the sensations he created inside her and she rolled her hips to match his movements.

"That's it, Sophie…look at me. Is this good?"

She nodded. "Yes…yes…so good." He kept his movements slow and careful, obviously intent on her pleasure, but it wasn't quite enough. She clutched him closer, wrapping one leg around his waist and burying her fingers in his hair. "What about you?" she gasped.

The corner of his mouth ticked up in a sexy little smile. "This is about you."

"This is about us."

"Us. I like the sound of that." He pressed his lips to hers, and shifted his weight, moving deeper within her.

She gasped against his lips as she arched up from the sofa, clenching impossibly tight around him. A glorious full-body shiver rippled through her.

A moment later, he buried his face in the crook of her neck and shuddered his own release. He dropped his head against her shoulder.

Sophie combed her hands through his hair as he panted, breath hot against her chest. Finally, his racing pulse slowed, and he rolled them over carefully. He tucked her hair behind her ear.

"Wow. That was…"

She smiled, brushing his hair back from his forehead. "Yeah. It was."

****

A breeze ruffled the gauzy white curtains in Sophie's windows. Late morning sun—very late morning—filtered into the room. Sam turned his head on the pillow and smiled. Sophie lay facing him, with the sheet pulled across her chest, still sound asleep. He brushed a lock of hair from her cheek, careful not to wake her, no matter how eager he might be to continue last night's activities. *She looks so peaceful. This is the most relaxed I've ever seen her…and I'm sure she can use the rest.*

One of the cats—he couldn't really tell them apart yet—blinked lazily at him from the foot of the bed, then washed its front paw and laid its head back down.

His gaze wandered the room he hadn't gotten a very good look at the night before. Touches of butter yellow and rose softened the blue and white color scheme. Framed photos covered the faded floral paper of one wall—Sophie growing lovelier year by year, from play clothes to graduation cap and gown—often accompanied by an older couple. Bonnie appeared in some of them. Sophie's glorious red hair splayed across her pillow formed the brightest splash of color in the room.

Worn paperbacks filled a low white bookcase, and a cozy cat bed sat in the corner, though Carb and Ginny had spent most of the night at the foot of the bed. Well, at least once they stopped talking…among other things…and fell asleep.

I could get used to waking up like this…

Her ball gown hung on the outside of the closet door, swathed in dry cleaner's plastic, ready for next Saturday. Beside him, Sophie inhaled softly. He turned his head on the pillow and saw her blinking sleep from her beautiful brown eyes. He propped up on his elbow and kissed her delicately, running his fingers through her hair.

"'Morning."

She smiled languidly. "Good morning yourself. What are you contemplating over there?"

He leaned over and kissed her shoulder, still playing with the ends of her hair. "I can't decide if you're more gorgeous dressed up for a fancy ball or just like this."

A delightful rosy blush spread over her cheeks. "You're not so bad yourself."

The tolling of a church bell drifted through the open windows.

"What time is it?"

He raised his arm automatically, then blinked at his bare wrist. "I don't know. I seem to have left my watch…somewhere." He leaned farther over, gaze focused on her. "Does it matter?"

She slipped her arm around his neck, stroking her fingers through his hair. "I suppose only if you're picky about what you call your meals."

"Oh?"

"Well, when we get up, will we be eating breakfast, brunch, or lunch?"

He settled over her, pressing her into the mattress. "How about dinner?"

"I like the way you think. Although, if we keep this up, you may need to go on another shopping excursion."

He kissed her lightly on the mouth. "That can be arranged."

"I should check my phone."

Sam pressed his lips to her throat. "It's Sunday." He tugged the sheet a bit lower, kissing the space between her breasts. Her skin was so soft—and so responsive to his lightest teasing touch.

"You have voice mail." He looked up at her.

She cupped his cheek in her hand, running her thumb over his lips. "I have responsibilities."

He kissed her forehead, then rolled off her. "Yeah, you do."

"Thank you for understanding."

He grinned and tucked her hair behind her ear. "I understand it's still Sunday, so five minutes to check your phone, and if there's nothing urgent, we go right back to relaxing."

"Deal."

Chapter Thirteen

Sophie grinned as she locked up her bike outside town hall Monday morning. Waking up beside Sam had been incredible on so many levels. It had been…a while since she indulged in adult recreation. She forgot how amazing it felt to be wrapped up in someone. Sam fit into her home in a way no one else had ever quite managed. Even Carb and Ginny adored him. They were grown adults—not college kids. They were talking everything through and not making thoughtless promises. They could make this work.

She pushed open the door and her mood evaporated instantly. Phones rang off the hook—bad enough Bonnie was fielding calls. She and Wilf answered each with a terse "no comment at this time." Wilf glanced up and waved her over to his desk.

She hurried across the room, dropping her bag on the floor. "What happened? I checked my phone right before I left home."

"I didn't want you distracted and getting in an accident. Come look at this." He indicated a newspaper on his desk.

A full-page, full-color ad stared back at her. *Research proves Northanger Holdings Waterfront Development Project is the future of Regency Bay.* An image of Finn in full SCUBA gear grinned, giving a cheerful thumbs-up. Nearby, Octavia floated on her back cradling her latest baby on her chest. It was the same photo she had on her desk. The one Sam took. The one he'd printed and framed and given her for a gift. The room tilted on its axis, and she grabbed the back of Wilf's guest chair.

"That's Finn."

Wilf nodded. "A member of the research team, apparently giving their support to Northanger's project."

"Hence about half of these phone calls," Bonnie said, hanging up the phone yet again.

Sophie tried to speak, but her mouth was bone dry. She licked her lips, trying to work up a little moisture. "Sam took that picture." She crumpled into the chair.

Wilf passed her a tall paper cup and she sipped a mouthful of tepid bitterness. Her hand shook as she set it down. *Please don't let me puke on his desk...*

"Which paper is this?"

"Marcus. Who the hell else would pull a stunt like this?"

"No comment," Bonnie snapped and slammed her phone down.

"I-I need to..." *Why is it so hard to speak? And why is there no oxygen in this room?*

Wilf covered her icy fingers with his big, warm hand. "You need to issue a statement."

Sophie blinked, then sucked in a breath, choking on air. Wilf squeezed her hand, grounding her enough to take deep, even breaths, filling her lungs with air instead of gulping spit.

"Let's go with 'no comment' until I can figure out what's going on."

"You should talk to Sam."

"I can't."

"Sophie, I know you like him, but—"

"No—it's not personal." The words burned like acid in her throat. "He's out on the Queen Caroline this morning, with Finn."

"They're diving with a team from the Smithsonian," Bonnie elaborated. "Most of the researchers are involved. They're on a tight schedule and no one will interrupt them unless it's something like Stan closing the harbor."

"Which he has no reason to do." Sophie flickered a glance out the window at the sickeningly perfect summer day. "I guess the first step is to discover how they got hold of Sam's picture." She grabbed the paper, taking a closer look. "This is high resolution—like an original file, not a bootleg copy. Could his room at the boarding house have been broken into? Maybe his laptop or a memory card was stolen?" *He was with me all weekend…anything could be missing from his room, and he might not realize it yet.*

Bonnie spun her chair to face her, ignoring the jangling phones. "If someone lifted a memory card, he might not have noticed. The things are the size of postage stamps."

Sophie rested her elbows on Wilf's desk and sank her head into her hands. *Breathe. Breathe for crissake. You're gonna pass out.* After a long moment she looked up. "Okay. Wilf, can you please call Margaret's for me and have them get someone else to cover my tours? This is going to take a day or two to sort out."

"At the very least," he agreed.

"Then we need to find out for sure who funded the ad and how they got their hands on the photo—"

The door opened and Darrell Masterson stood

backlit in the entry, smiling in all of his three-piece-suit-and-silk-tie glory.

Satan must smile like that when he's made a really good deal.

"I can answer your question, Mayor Bennet. Northanger Holdings purchased and approved the ad. The photograph belongs to us. It was taken by a photographer we have on retainer. His name is Samuel Trowbridge. I believe you're acquainted. I can even provide copies of the receipts if you like."

****

Sam pushed open the door of the Anchor well past his usual dinner time. He should have called Sophie, but if he didn't eat some actual food soon he'd fall on his face. Whoever decided energy bars make good meals needed their head examined. He glanced around for a flash of ginger hair. Perhaps she was here. Bonnie might have dragged her out for dinner.

The familiar, homey atmosphere of enticing food aromas and good fellowship washed over him. Patrons turned with greetings on their lips for the newcomers. Greetings that were never uttered. Conversation died away until the muted mutterings of the TV set and the beeps and bells of the pinball machine were the only sounds in the room. Every eye focused on him. He stopped short in the doorway and Finn walked right into him.

" 'Evening, Finn," Daisy called from behind the bar, wiping her hands on a ragged old towel decorated with the faded remnants of the beer logo with the big horses.

A chair scraped across the floor, deafeningly loud in the unnatural silence.

Sam glanced at Finn, who shrugged.

"Hey, Daisy. Is the kitchen still open?"

"For you, Finn? Sure. What can I get you?"

"Um, well…we'd like a couple burgers. Or whatever's easy. We were out on Queenie all day—"

"No. I'll get you whatever you want, Finn." She jerked her chin toward Sam. "Whatever he wants, we're all sold out."

Sam scanned the room warily. The sea of accusing glares no longer focused on him. The owners of said glares had pointedly turned their backs. "Daisy? What's wrong?"

"Why don't you ask your good friend Mr. Darrell Masterson for a recommendation? His company owns plenty of restaurant chains."

"Who?"

Bonnie hopped down from a barstool, face set and pale. She held out a crumpled sheet of newspaper.

Sam unfolded it. "I don't understand."

Finn peered over his shoulder. "Neither do I. I never agreed to my likeness appearing in a newspaper ad. And I never said—"

"We know it wasn't you." Bonnie laid a hand on Finn's arm.

Sam gripped the paper so hard the edges shredded. "Well, it sure as hell wasn't me."

Bonnie snapped her ever-present gum. "Yeah, it was. You work for Northanger Holdings. They own all the pictures you took. We thought—*Sophie* thought—you were on our side. Thanks a lot." She turned and led Finn back to her seat.

"No, I don't." *Why won't she believe me?* "I work For Pemberley Films."

"Which is a subsidiary of Northanger Holdings,"

Daisy informed him. "Maybe you should have done your homework. Now I'd like you to leave my property. Your bosses don't own it yet."

Chapter Fourteen

Sam sat on the edge of the creaky iron-framed bed, staring at the floor. In the way of small towns, news spread with a swiftness that left high speed internet connections in the dust. The neighbors upstairs were unusually stompy tonight. And judging from the rhythmic pounding on the other side of the wall, the guests next door were engaged in the sort of activity he wouldn't be experiencing again any time soon. Neither was sleeping a possibility with all the racket. Not to mention the picture frames bouncing against the wall over his bed. *There's a concussion waiting to happen.*

The dry cleaners had delivered his costume, fresh and pressed for a ball he suspected he was no longer welcome to attend, and he had a voice mail from Sparrow about the fancy reproduction shoes he no longer needed. The local florist called and cancelled the nosegay he'd ordered for Sophie for the ball. Evidently, they were sold out of pink rosebuds. And ferns. And baby's breath.

When he awoke this morning, he had a place in this town. He had colleagues who respected him and an incredible woman he thought was falling for him as hard as he fell for her. How the hell did this happen in twelve hours?

He pulled out his phone and thumbed through his contacts. Nothing from Sophie. Swallowing the tattered remnants of his pride, he dialed his brother. Who of course answered on the first ring.

"Kevin Trowbridge speaking."

Sam rolled his eyes. *As if there isn't such a thing as caller ID.* "Hey, Kevin…it's me. I need your help. Maybe Maisie's, too." An explosive sigh gusted through the connection, and he jerked the phone away from his ear.

"It's about time. What did you decide on, law school or business? Of course we'll help you, but you've been out of college for a while. You should consider a good prep course—"

"Kev—no. I'm not going back to school."

"You know, you're lucky you have parents willing to foot the bill for you. Do you know how many people graduate with a mountain of student debt?"

"Can we not rehash this right now? I need help from someone who understands business and law. If you want to argue, I can go online and look for pro bono services."

The line went quiet. "Are you in trouble?"

"No! I mean, I don't think so." Another deafening beat of silence. "Maybe?"

"All right. Hang on a second." There were shuffling and rustling sounds—probably Kevin grabbing a pen and pad. "Okay. I put this on hands-free so I can take notes. Tell me everything."

****

"Well? How much trouble am I in?"

One of Kevin's patented "thoughtful" sighs sounded through the phone. "I don't know. Maybe not any. You acted in good faith and a competent lawyer can work with that."

"You think I need a lawyer?"

Another sigh, different in tone. He must still practice them in front of a mirror. Must make Maisie as nuts as it always made him.

"I'm not sure yet. Email me your contract and release form and I'll go over the language."

"Thanks, Kev. Really."

"One good thing about this gig-based lifestyle of yours—you can leave in a few weeks. Where are you headed next? What do you have planned?"

"I…nothing. I wasn't planning on leaving. I've been looking for another job in the area so I could stay on in Regency Bay."

"Why?"

"Because I like it here. I have friends—"

A snort instead of a sigh this time. "From what you told me, your friends may be in short supply."

Sam scrunched his eyes shut against the pounding in his temples. "I love this place. I love the old-fashioned boardwalk and the cutting-edge conservation, and I love the damn otters."

"The otters, huh?" Kevin chuckled. "What's her name, Sam?"

"Shut up."

"There's an entire coast full of beaches and boardwalks and conservation you could take pictures of. What's so special about this place?"

What wasn't special? "It could have been just another washed-up, imploded old resort town, but the people who live here got together and cleaned up their beach and their bay and committed to restoring their town. What they've accomplished is extraordinary. And they deserve better than to be bought out by a big conglomerate that's planning to trash their hard work."

"And what's her name?" Kevin asked again, quietly.

This time, Sam sighed gustily. "Sophie. Her name is Sophie. She's beautiful and smart and dedicated to this town—"

"And you're in love with her," Maisie interjected.

Right. Hands-free. So much for a private conversation. "Yeah, I am. But right now, she thinks I betrayed her trust and her town."

"Have you spoken to her?" Maisie asked.

"No."

"Don't you think you should?"

"I'm not sure she'll see me."

"If she's as special as you say, I think she will."

****

Wilf pushed open the office door, extra-large recyclable coffee cup in hand. "You're here early."

Sophie scanned the Vesuvius of paperwork scattered across her desk, then reached for another folder. "There's a busy weekend coming up. Have any of the conference guests arrived yet?"

"They're starting to trickle in. Some of the writers have book signings scheduled in town and at the bookstore out at the mall. A couple of vendors are scheduled to arrive today to set up. Your friend Sparrow is at the Netherfield until after the reenactor's event."

"Good. No dire weather forecasts or supply issues?"

"Not to my knowledge." He balanced a more files on top of her already overflowing inbox. "You still need to make an appearance at the ball Saturday. With or without escort."

She glanced at the plastic-wrapped gown hanging on the back of her door. "I know." She refocused her attention on her paperwork.

113

"Have you talked to him?"

"No."

"You should." He set down her morning coffee. "We're still sorting through the paperwork. It's quite possible he didn't know—"

She shook her head. "Doesn't matter."

"Of course it matters."

"It doesn't. It's the way things look. People were already commenting on us spending time together. Now it turns out he's working for Northanger? I'm the mayor. Regency Bay comes first. It has to, or what did the town elect me for?"

"By 'people' you mean Marcus."

"Who manages to sell papers in this town. Regardless of what we think of him, people read what he says. And you know the next thing he'll do is start looking for a candidate to endorse for my job who'll be delighted to hand over our town to Northanger Holdings."

"I think you overestimate his influence—and underestimate the regard the people hold you in. I think we can put off worrying about reelection for a bit."

She snorted. "Yeah, 'cuz you're not the one sitting behind this desk."

"No, but I'll probably be out of a job if Marcus and his cronies take over."

"Thanks for reminding me." She sank her head into her hands. "Ugh. What day is this, anyway?"

"Still only Tuesday, I'm afraid. Look, Sophie…maybe Sam could have been a little more diligent in his choice of employer, but I've seen the way he looks at you—and the way you look at him. That kind of connection is too precious to throw away."

"Wilf…"

He leaned his considerable bulk on the corner of her desk. "You're not a pair of teenagers screwing around for summer break. You're adults. And when adults become close, the way you and Sam have, a conversation is owed."

She scowled mutinously. "You're not my dad."

"No, but I'm his friend and I know what he'd have to say in this instance. Talk to Sam." He headed for the door.

"A frank and open discussion."

Wilf turned with his hand on the doorknob. "Pardon?"

"That's what Sam promised. That he wouldn't just disappear on me. That we'd talk things out."

"Don't you think you owe him the same courtesy?"

****

Sparrow was redressing one of the mannequins on display in front of their temporary shop in the Netherfield when Sophie walked in, the plastic wrapped blue gown draped carefully over her arm. They'd changed their hair to streaks of vivid blue and green and wore a matching tie-dyed sleeveless dress that clung to their lanky frame. Color-shifting nail polish Bonnie would adore completed the look.

Sophie cleared her throat quietly. "I came to return this."

Sparrow turned from their display, towering a few inches over Sophie. "But why? It looks wonderful on you."

"It's lovely. Truly. I was super careful wearing it and I had it dry-cleaned. I'm sure you'll have no trouble finding a buyer and I'm happy to pay whatever the going rate is for the rental."

"No." Sparrow reluctantly took the dress. "It was a loan. I meant it to be a gift."

"I know, and it's so kind of you but…my old gown holds a lot of bad memories. I thought this one would be a fresh start…"

Sparrow stuck the hanger on the end of the nearest rack and took Sophie's hand. "Oh, honey—what happened? You looked so happy the night of the ball."

Tears prickled at Sophie's eyes, and she blinked furiously to hold them back. "I was, but…things…didn't work out." She swallowed a lump in her throat and pasted on a watery smile. "I'm sure you've heard the gossip going around."

"It's not my place to get involved in local affairs, but you're the best thing that ever happened to this town. And it's not just the sales I get from your events." They waved a hand vaguely at themselves. "I feel safe in this community. I can walk anywhere dressed however I want or stop in to Pride and Promises and no one hassles me."

Sophie squeezed their hand. "I'm glad. I want this to be a good place for everyone who wants to live or visit here, and it won't be if a big corporation comes in and takes over the whole waterfront."

"I understand. But…I only met your fella a few times, but he seems like a good guy. Are you sure he's really on board with that company?"

The array of beautiful dresses blurred into a smear of rainbow colors before Sophie's eyes, and she squeezed them shut for a moment before answering. "It's complicated. Even if he had no idea, people have seen us together and it's been noted by the press. I must consider—"

"The way things look?" Sparrow shook their head. "I used to worry about that, too. For a long time, I strictly sold online because I didn't think customers would accept someone who looks like me creating historically correct Regency and Federal era apparel. The theatrical stuff, sure, but hand-sewn buttonholes or the correct style cap a middle-aged woman would wear at home in the morning?"

"You have a fantastic reputation with the cosplayers and the reenactors—not to mention the brides."

"Yes, but it took me a long time to let them see who they were really dealing with. I was terrified the first time I appeared at a historical event in costume."

Sophie's curiosity got the better of her. "What happened? I mean…if you don't mind my asking?"

Sparrow shrugged. "Someone asked my source for the fabric of my ensemble, someone else inquired about hiring me to costume a Christmas panto, and word got out that I had the finest partlets anyone had seen at that event, and I sold out of all of them and took a bunch of orders for more. So, it's possible to be you and still have the career you want."

"Yeah, except I can be voted out of office."

"You could. I mean, you're going to, eventually. Term limits are a thing. At some point you'll need to consider what comes next." They offered a one-shouldered shrug. "Be easier to think about with the right partner."

"I just met him this summer."

"Sometimes it happens that way. Look, I don't pretend to know either of you very well, but he doesn't strike me as a bad guy. And I think it speaks for his innocence that he's still here. You should listen to what he has to say."

"He deserves a conversation."

"He does." Sparrow grabbed the blue gown from the rack with a saucy wink. "I'll hold this aside, in case you change your mind."

Chapter Fifteen

The front desk clerk at the Netherfield glanced in his direction as Sam entered the lobby, then pointedly returned to folding key packets. No one greeted him or even smiled as he made his way to the conference room that housed Sparrow's temporary shop. No way would he make it through a whole month of this.

Sparrow grinned when they saw him coming. Today's ensemble included bike shorts, platform sandals which added four more inches to their height, and a T-shirt featuring a pair of sequined red boots. "Sam—hi! I'm glad you got my message. Your shoes arrived—I even threw in a pair of proper white silk stockings, instead of whatever the heck you wore to the last party. The shoes will fit better, and I won't cringe every time you pass me."

"Thanks, Sparrow, but I'm afraid I won't be needing them." He raised a hand before they could get in a word. "You keep the money. The shoes were a special order, and I wouldn't mess with a small vendor. I have average size feet. I'm sure you'll find another buyer." He rubbed the back of his neck with one hand. "You've probably heard…"

They glanced down at the floor, then back at him. "I've heard some stuff, and I'm truly sorry. Look…I don't live here, and I know it's not my business, but you're hardly the picture of a mustache-twirling villain."

He huffed out a hollow shadow of a laugh. "Well, thanks for that. I think. For whatever the hell it's worth, I took this job in good faith. I honestly thought I was doing something good for the community."

Sparrow leaned a hip against the table they used as a checkout counter and crossed their arms over their chest. "Road to hell and all that."

Sam nodded. "I didn't know Northanger owned the film company. I swear. And I don't know how to fix any of it."

"I'd say telling the truth is a good place to start."

"So would I, if the whole town hadn't already convicted me, without benefit of trial or jury. I mean, I'm glad everyone's rallying behind Sophie—she deserves their full support, after everything she's done for this town—"

"But it hurts when no one will give you a chance to defend yourself? Yeah, I know something about that."

"It's just…no one will give me the time of day. None of the restaurants will serve me, so I've been driving out to the mall, or the thruway rest stop for fast food, except now my car needs charging but somehow there's no EV stations available anywhere in town." He stopped and heaved a full-body sigh Kevin would envy. "I think the only reason my room at the boarding house is still being serviced is so it's in good condition to rent to someone else once they find an excuse to evict me."

"I know something about that, too," Sparrow murmured.

"So how do you…keep going? When no one will listen to you? I mean…I know it's not the same thing, and I don't pretend to understand what your life has been like…"

"You speak your truth. And you keep speaking it until someone listens. And honey? The ones who listen? Those are the keepers." They touched his wrist lightly and winked. "Now, if I was you, the first person I'd want to talk to is Sophie."

"She won't take my calls."

"Seriously? That's what's stopping you? Her office is listed on the town map! And I'm pretty sure you know where she lives."

"And that's not stalking?"

"If she tells you to go to hell after hearing you out and you stick around, then yeah, it's stalking. But I don't think she's the sort to give you the boot without at least hearing your side."

"Me neither."

Sparrow flapped their hands at him. "Well? She's not hiding in my dressing room! So go on out there and find her and tell her your truth and see what happens."

"Thanks, Sparrow. Really."

"I'll hold these shoes in the back in case you change your mind...along with a certain blue gown. There're two more costumed events this season. You might still need them."

****

Sophie's phone chirped from amidst the clutter of her desk. She unearthed it and checked the caller ID before answering. She winced, then touched the screen.

"Hi, Mom." She put the phone on hands-free, and her mother's cheerful chatter filled the office.

"Hello, darling! I've found the most wonderful new kitchen accessory—it's an indoor composter. It's odorless and can hold a week's worth of kitchen scraps so I don't have to go outside to the bin. I ordered a few for the store. I think they'll sell quite nicely here, come winter."

"Mom, it's California. Stepping outside to the compost bin in winter isn't a big deal."

"Maybe not for young folks, but I know I don't want to go outside if it's raining or windy. I think there's a market for it."

"Of course, Mom. I'm sure you're right." She pinched the bridge of her nose. Just get it over with. "So why the pressing need to tell me about this new acquisition? Who told you?"

"Who told me what, darling?"

"Mom."

A soft sigh sounded through the connection. "Well, you know your father and I only read the Clarion, but we couldn't help hearing a lot of talk about some dreadful young man who's been secretly working for that awful company."

And there it is. "Okay, Mom, first, his name is Sam. He's not dreadful and I'm not sure he knew he was really working for Northanger."

"How could he not know who he works for?"

"Because companies own other companies. It's a thing. About half the brands in the supermarket are owned by one conglomerate."

"Well, a supermarket conglomerate didn't jilt my little girl."

"Mom, he didn't jilt me. I'm not a little girl, and by the way, nobody says jilt. Anyway…"

"Anyway what?"

Deep breath. In through the nose, out through the mouth. "If anything, I'm the one who's avoiding him."

"Why? If he's so not dreadful and he didn't jilt

you?"

"Because I'm the mayor and there's no such thing as privacy in a town this size. How does it look for me to date a guy who's apparently working for the company with plans to bulldoze our entire waterfront?"

"So, you were dating him? Another summer guy? Sweetheart…"

"Mom, I'm not a college kid reeling in the throes of my first romance. I'm all grown up and I went into this with my eyes wide open." The silence from the other end of the connection was deafening. "Well, at least as far as him being a summer guy."

"You really like this young man?"

"Yeah."

"And you think he's innocent?"

Sophie straightened in her chair. "Yes, I do."

"Well, then, I think you need to have a conversation with him."

"Mom, it's not so simple."

"Oh, sweetheart…of course it is."

****

The sky was still dark when Sophie pulled into the lot behind town hall Thursday morning. The beam of her headlights startled one of the local strays. The black and white cow kitty froze for a moment, caught in the act of stalking something with a long skinny tail that streaked away. The cat hissed, then bounded away into the shadows in pursuit of its lost prey.

Her key ring jingled merrily as she hunted for the front door key she so seldom used. Wilf almost always beat her to the office, but today she'd given up on tossing and turning and headed to work, planning to make inroads on the mountain of disaster looming on her desk.

No phones, no meetings...I have a couple hours alone—

A dark shape stirred on the bench beside the front door. The boardwalk was well patrolled, so vagrants weren't usually a problem, but *of course* this was the cherry on top of the week from hell and *of course* no place was open at this unholy hour she could duck into, and *of course* whoever it was had already spotted her. Adrenaline spiked through her. Heart racing and hands shaking, she fumbled in her bag for her phone.

The person on the bench rubbed a hand over their face. "Sophie?"

"Sam?" The tension washed out of her like the morning tide running back out to sea. Whatever happened between them, he'd never hurt her. She *knew* it in her bones. "What on earth are you doing here?"

"Um..." He cleared his throat and tried again. "Waiting for you?"

"All night?"

"Yeah. If this was one of those horrid Gothic novels, this would be the part where the dark, brooding anti-hero wanders the moors, consumed with guilt over the destruction his evil deeds hath wrought."

She arched a brow, pressing her lips together to restrain the laughter trying to bubble up. "Dramatic, much?"

His shoulders dropped and the corner of his mouth tilted up ever so slightly. "Maybe. I...apparently got locked out of the boarding house last night. But I really need to talk to you, and every time I came by, Bonnie or Wilf said you were either on a call or in a meeting."

Wait—wasn't Wilf firmly in the "you need to speak to him" camp? She shook her head to dispel the cobwebs. "I'm the mayor and there's a pretty big event happening this weekend, in case you missed all the advertisements."

"I know." He shoved his hands deep in his pockets. "So, since I had no place to spend the night, I figured I'd wait for you."

"You were out here, all night, on this bench?"

He shrugged.

"I went by the boarding house last night. The front door worked fine, and I saw your car in the lot. You didn't answer when the desk clerk called your room."

"I didn't answer because I wasn't there. My car needs to be charged, but I can't find an EV station to plug into. It hasn't budged from that spot in a couple days. I also can't find any place in town willing to sell me dinner, so I took the bus to the mall. When I got back, I'd been locked out." He scuffed the toe of his sneaker against the worn planks of the boardwalk. "For whatever the hell it's worth, Sophie, I didn't know. I swear."

"I believe you." Hands steadier, she unlocked the front door and switched off the alarm. "Come on in. You can clean up in the washroom while I start coffee."

He raked his hand through his unruly hair. "Thanks."

****

Sam followed the scent of coffee to the small break room off the lobby. Sophie sat at the table, turning a "Greetings from Regency Bay" mug between her hands. Another sat at the place opposite. He sat and warmed his hands on his own mug—it might be August, but the night breeze was brisk.

"I apologize," Sophie murmured without looking up from her cup.

"Think you stole my line." He took a sip of coffee, not really tasting it, even though she'd added some vanilla creamer.

She inhaled sharply. "No—I should have taken your calls, at the very least. I had a knee-jerk reaction. 'Oh look, I got burned by another summer guy.' Only this time, it wasn't just me—"

He reached across the table and touched the back of her hand. "Hey—you have every right to be upset. I know how much this town means to you. And I know how bad it must have looked. I'm sorry. I am so, so sorry." *I've never wanted to hold anyone as much as I want to hold you right now.* "Tell me how I can make things right between us."

She huffed out a sound somewhere between a laugh and a sob. "I'm not sure you can." She blinked her eyes furiously, trying to contain a sudden shimmer of tears. One overflowed and slid down her cheek.

His heart twisted in his chest for causing them. "Sophie, I care for you, and I think you care for me, too. I honestly didn't know Northanger owned the film company. I want to fix this."

She reclaimed her hand and scrubbed her eyes. "If it was just you and me, maybe we could get past this. But it's not just us. I'm the mayor. Everything I do is visible. I've been fighting this takeover tooth and nail and if it looks like I'm—"

"Sleeping with the enemy?"

"God, that sounds so tawdry." She swallowed hard, then met his gaze. "Look, I wanted to clear the air between us, but I just…I can't be seen with you."

He winced. The thought of walking away from Sophie—from the possibility of *them* they'd discussed only a couple of days ago—was a swift gut punch. "I understand. I'll stay out of your way as much as I can. Hell, I might be gone before Labor Day."

"Why? What happened? I thought you had a contract through the end of the summer?"

"I do, but the company's been getting a ton of letters from lawyers threatening suits, saying I obtained permission to take photographs of their clients' persons and property under false pretenses. Their paperwork is ironclad so I expect it's more a nuisance than anything else, but the complaints, coupled with the fact no one will let me film anything anymore...well, if I don't submit new photographs, I don't expect they'll be footing my boarding house bill much longer."

"I'm sorry. Can I talk to anyone? Make this easier somehow? If people understand you aren't to blame—"

"No. Like you said, you need to protect the town. You have to distance yourself."

"What will you do?"

He shrugged. "Move on. Find another project. Do a better job of investigating my next employer."

"Can anyone...will there be legal repercussions for you?"

"My brother and his wife are sifting through the whole mess. They think I'll be okay, as long as—"

"As long as you don't make waves with Northanger?"

"Yeah."

Chapter Sixteen

The romance writers' retreat ranked right up there with Valentine's Day, as far as forms of personal hell. Except Valentine's Day at least held the promise of half price chocolate the next day. Everything about the event mocked Sophie's battered heart, from the "swoon worthy" displays in the bookstore windows, to the ads for the moonlight champagne cruise, and of course, all the hoopla for the grand ball Saturday night. Where she was still expected to make an appearance. And of course, Wednesday's beach movie had been her favorite fifties-style musical rom-com, which would have been so much fun to watch, snuggled in Sam's arms and singing along with the familiar songs. Instead, she'd gone home with a bag full of work files.

Bonnie's constant stream of texts and emails from Finn didn't help, either. *She's my best friend and I love her, but if I hear one more allusion to their plans for after the ball, I am going to lose it.*

The few tours she'd managed to squeeze in this week were a special form of torture. All her favorite haunts were colored with memories of showing them to Sam.

Sitting in a hotel dining room at a lace-draped banquet table smiling and pretending to drink tea was more painful than the proverbial rack or thumbscrews. A cup of dead leaves, a plateful of pitiful little morsels sprouting more leaves masquerading as sandwiches, and the luncheon's keynote speaker prattling on about "black moments" and "resolutions" and "happily ever afters" set her teeth on edge.

The woman beside her nudged her gently with an elbow. "Your eyes are glazing over, dear."

Sophie straightened in her chair. "Sorry. It's the busiest time of year for me. I have a lot on my mind."

The silvery-haired lady smiled, displaying a merry set of dimples. "You seem a bit out of your element."

She poked at one of the tiny sandwiches on her plate. Nope. Nothing resembling protein hiding in there. "Honestly...I'd kill for a nice messy burger. I can't remember the last time I ate a decent meal."

"And I'd like a rather large glass of red wine. Still, when one writes Regency romance—or resides in a town called Regency Bay—one is expected to show a certain level of enthusiasm for balls and tea parties."

Sophie offered a one-shouldered shrug. "I've always focused more on the 'Bay' part than the 'Regency' stuff."

"And none of us would be here if you hadn't cleaned up the bay and restored the beautiful beach." She winked at Sophie. "But it's always good to leave a little room for romance—of one sort or another. I'm Terry, by the way."

"Sophie Bennet."

"The lady mayor responsible for returning the otters to the bay."

The speaker switched to the topic of "creatively reinterpreting history," sparking a good deal of angry muttering throughout the room.

Terry rolled her eyes. "Sometimes I wonder why I attend these things. There's room for all our stories. No need for all these ruffled feathers."

Sophie dropped the unappetizing sandwich back on her plate. "How do you do it? I mean, how do you keep writing these stories about love and romance and happy endings, as if—"

Terry smiled gently. "As if there was no sadness or upset in the world? Oh, my dear…why do you think we tell these stories, if not to offer a bit of escape, and the hope that there's a happy ending out there for everyone?" She patted the back of Sophie's hand. "Even for lady mayors of a decidedly scientific mindset. You'd make an excellent character, you know."

Sophie smiled at her new friend uncertainly. *She's kidding, right?*

****

Like the cosplayers' ball earlier in the season, the romance writers' party spilled out the doors of the Longbourn onto the boardwalk. Although his shorts and T-shirt were wildly out of place among the costumes and evening wear, Sam edged through the crowd, desperately hoping for a glimpse of Sophie.

I need to tell her I'm leaving…and I'll be back. Kev's idea will work. They always do. He's the brains of the family.

Bonnie caught his eye first, wearing her blinding lime green satin gown. And there she was—a pale shadow clad in a dark blue gown. *Must be her old dress—the one she wore when that guy dumped her at New Year's. Way to go, Sam.* Wilf hovered nearby, resplendent in a coat and tie, along with an older couple he recognized from pictures in her home. They formed a protective cluster around Sophie, shielding her from press and gossip mongers.

He swallowed bile. *I'm glad she has them, but it's my fault she needs them.*

Someone tapped his shoulder, and he turned and found himself eye to tactical vest with one of the security guards brought in for big events. The fellow loomed over him, one hand resting on the tazer at his belt.

"Sir, the manager on duty has instructed me to escort you from the hotel."

"Look, I'm not trying to crash the party—really. I just need to speak to the mayor for a moment."

"I'm sorry, sir, but the owners are involved in legal action against you and your employers and you're not welcome on the property."

A crowd gathered between him and Sophie, locals whispering behind their hands to visitors. Their hostility crept over him in a palpable wave. "I don't want any trouble, okay? I'll go. But if I can't speak to her, could you at least give her a message? Please?"

"Sir, I suggest you send an email or a text. Right now, I need you to leave the building, or the staff will call the police." His hand rested more firmly on the tazer, and he edged Sam inexorably toward the door.

The last thing I need is to get arrested. His shoulders slumped as he turned toward the exit. Then a flash of blue-streaked hair caught his eye. Finally, a possible ally. He waved frantically. "Sparrow! Tell Sophie I'm going to Sacramento!"

Sparrow frowned and cupped a hand around their ear.

Dammit, they can't hear me. "Please, can I just—?"

The guard clicked his radio. "Front desk, come in please." He strode forward, herding Sam toward the exit.

"Tell her my brother has an idea!" He tried to dig in

his heels. "Make sure she knows I'm coming back!"

The grand old double doors slammed shut in his face. His feet dragged as he walked to his newly-recharged car. He didn't notice the hotel's lights flicker and go out as he pulled onto Austen Boulevard and headed out of town.

Chapter Seventeen

"I'm really sorry, Sophie. I thought he said Sacramento, but I couldn't hear over the crowd. Security was super serious about throwing him out, and then all the lights went out. Maybe he sent you a text or something. Have you checked?"

"I dropped my phone somewhere in the confusion after the power outage. It hasn't turned up yet. Anyway...he probably did say Sacramento. His brother works there." *And he has a standing offer from his folks. A whole new career. Guess he decided to cut his losses.* Sophie manufactured a smile and laid her hand on Sparrow's arm. "It's okay. I think it's the universe trying to tell me this...relationship...was never meant to be." A soft sigh escaped her lips. "Like my vision for this town."

Sparrow set their hands on their hips. "Honey, now you're just feeling sorry for yourself. Everything worked out fine on Saturday. The party moved outside to the boardwalk, generators—which I understand were purchased as part of the emergency protocols you put in place—were set up, and everyone had a blast."

"Yeah, but you can't run an entire hotel on generators for more than a couple days. The Longbourn is an old building. The owners knew sooner or later the electrical system would need a full overhaul. It's going to be a huge cash outlay."

"But it's almost the end of the season. Can't they

manage repairs to get them through a few more weeks? Then do a proper renovation during the off season?"

Sophie shook her head. "They have weddings booked for the fall. And the new Halloween event is based on the idea of having all four hotels running at peak capacity. And…"

"And?"

"The Longbourn is located in the center of the boardwalk. If they sell—"

"If that company gets a foothold on the Longbourn site, it splits the boardwalk in half. Damn."

Damn, indeed.

****

A soft tap at the door woke Sam. Sort of.

"Hey, Sam, you alive in there?"

He blinked blearily, the white walls and dark wood accents of Kevin's house coming into focus. Kevin and Maisie lived the parentally-approved good life— beautiful brick house with a lawn on a charming, tree-lined street in East Sacramento. The place was spacious enough for their soon-to-be-expanding family, with room for two home offices, a nursery, and even included a well-appointed "mother-in-law" apartment over the garage. The perfect place to stash a dead-beat brother-in-law.

"Sam?"

"Sorry, Maisie," he called through the door. He rubbed his face and cleared his throat. "What can I do for you?"

"Kevin's left for the office. Why don't you come down and I'll make you breakfast?"

He flushed guiltily. "You don't have to cook for me."

She chuckled. "Junior wants scrambled eggs and he's willing to share with his favorite uncle." A beat, then: "Come on. You drove all Saturday night and slept most of Sunday. You need to come out and be social and eat something."

The jump start from roadside assistance had been enough to get him out of town, at least as far as a parking garage where he could properly charge his car. He'd arrived at his brother's home at an obscene hour Sunday morning. *At least they let me sleep before the inquisition.* "I'm Junior's favorite uncle, huh?"

"Favorite uncle, only uncle—same difference. Come on…everything will look better after a shower and a cup of coffee."

He sat up, missing the familiar squeak of the iron bedframe in his room at the boarding house. "You have great faith in the restorative powers of caffeine."

"I wouldn't know. I haven't touched the stuff in seven months. Shower, then get your butt down to the kitchen before Junior and I eat everything."

"Yes, ma'am." He swung his legs over the side of the bed and glanced at the untidy jumble of bags he'd dropped in the corner. *Where the hell did I leave my toiletries?* He huffed out a weary breath and headed for the en suite bathroom. Although the apartment was nominally his space, and they never disturbed his belongings, it was always fresh and clean whenever he arrived. And indeed—Maisie had stocked it with all the standard guest supplies—towels, TP, soap—God bless amazing sisters-in-law.

He turned on the water, again jarred by the lack of clanging and creaking as the water heated. He discarded his forty-eight-hour old shorts and T-shirt and stepped under the jets. Of course, the last time he'd had a shower with decent water pressure had been at Sophie's. In true Regency Bay fashion, they'd shared "to conserve water." Not that conservation of any sort had been on either of their minds…He scrubbed a little harder than necessary, trying to erase the memories of her lithe body moving against his. How had everything gone so wrong so fast?

****

Sam followed the enticing aroma of fresh coffee down the back stairs to the large, open-plan kitchen. A collection of bright copper pans hung from a rack over the center island and a full suite of state-of-the-art appliances gleamed from the marble-topped counters.

Maisie perched on one of the bar stools beside the island, baby belly notwithstanding, sipping a mug of fragrant herbal tea. "Help yourself," she invited, gesturing to a large skillet keeping warm on the back of the stove.

"Thanks." He grabbed a plate and loaded it with scrambled eggs and bacon. A mug of glorious steaming caffeine waited in the fancy coffee maker. A bottle of vanilla syrup and one of French vanilla creamer stood nearby. "You're the best, Maisie."

Maisie tucked a lock of strawberry blonde hair behind her ear and scooped up a spoonful of eggs. She chewed and swallowed while he added cheese and a sprinkle of black pepper to his own plate.

"So, tell me about her."

He took a gulp of coffee, then set the mug down, the taste chokingly bitter in his mouth. "Sophie's smart and funny and beautiful and right now she thinks I betrayed her and her town. Or at the very least, I was incredibly stupid in my choice of employers."

Maisie turned her mug in her hands, then took a sip. "Have you spoken to her? Because I can't picture someone so wonderful who you learned to care for so quickly judging you without even hearing you out."

"It's complicated. She's the mayor, so everything she does is in the spotlight. So even if she believes I'm innocent, it looks bad for her if she's seen with me, when the whole town's convinced I conned them. It could cost her re-election."

"And does she? Believe you're innocent, I mean?"

"I think so. At least, she doesn't think I willingly made a deal with the devil."

"And is her political career more important than whatever the two of you have together?"

He pushed his eggs around his plate. "She's good for the town and the people who live there. I can't mess up everyone's lives just because I want to be with her."

"And what about what she wants?"

"Sophie's lived in Regency Bay her whole life. Her folks live there. The place is in her blood. She'll always put the town first. It's what makes her such a great mayor."

"So, all you have to do is prove your innocence to the town and win her back."

"Oh, that's all?" He turned on his stool and faced his placidly smiling sister-in-law. "And how do you propose I accomplish that?"

She grinned. "Not alone, that's how."

****

Sam perched on the edge of one of the leather-upholstered chairs in Kevin's home office, turning a can of beer in his hands. "What did you find out?"

"Well, Pemberley Films is indeed a subsidiary of

Northanger Holdings. It's buried pretty deep. You'd have to be looking specifically for the connection to stumble onto it. There's nothing wrong with that, per se. Companies own other companies. People form companies for specific projects."

Maisie leaned forward in her own chair, curled around her baby bump. "Like making a movie?"

Kevin nodded. "And tons of movies are proposed that never end up being made. Sam, you didn't do anything wrong. You took a job gathering background material for a proposed film. You acted in good faith."

"But I've ultimately been getting paid by Darrell Masterson and Northanger Holdings."

Kevin shook his head. "Your paychecks are from Pemberley Films. There's no reason why you would have looked any farther than that. It's okay."

"It's not okay."

Maisie reached over and squeezed his arm. "Hey. One step at a time."

"I need to fix this. There's gotta be something—"

"My brother, the superhero," Kevin muttered, shaking his head. "Why's this so important to you?"

Heat crept up the back of his neck. Before he could formulate words—

"Because he's in love," Maisie interjected with the particular sort of smugness only a very pregnant, born matchmaker could pull off.

He pressed his lips together, but didn't deny it.

Kevin eyed them both but selected another file folder. "Okay…if you really want to do this…the other name you gave me? Darrell Masterson? He was the closer on another big development. Same type of deal—quiet seaside town, lots of small, outdated businesses."

"And?"

"And Masterson swooped in, snatched up some faltering businesses and got a toehold in the town. Once he had an in, it was easy enough to buy out enough neighboring businesses and land to break ground on a fancy, all-inclusive resort."

A worried crinkle appeared between Maisie's eyes. "I'm guessing this didn't end well for the town."

Kevin shook his head, consulting his notes. "The resort facilities were too expensive for residents to patronize. The town is just a little too far from airports and major train terminals to attract guests. It was a sleepy little place serving a trickle of tourists who went there for some fishing, a little antiquing, a weekend in a quaint B&B...not the sort of audience that wanted or could afford a big splashy resort."

Sam's fingers clenched into the beer can. "What..." He cleared his throat and tried again. "What happened?"

"The resort went bust after a couple of seasons. Masterson's company—Seaside Holdings—sold it off. Right now, there's a big box store, a couple of franchise hotels that change hands every couple of seasons, and a lot of vacant real estate."

"What else?"

Kevin met his gaze gravely. "A lot of people unemployed or in dead-end jobs."

Sam slumped forward, resting his forehead on one hand. "Pollution?" he mumbled, swallowing bile.

"Yeah."

"But was there anything illegal about the transactions?" Maisie asked.

Kevin sighed—one of the big, full-body ones he usually reserved for courtrooms. "Not as far as I can tell."

"Just because it's legal doesn't make it right." Sam crunched the beer can tighter. "I need something Sophie can use to save Regency Bay from this guy."

Kevin closed the file folder and tapped it on his blotter, straightening the contents. "I'll keep looking, but this seems to be everything available in public records, and it all appears to be in order. I can't go to my boss and say my brother thinks this developer is shady." He spread his hands and shrugged slightly. "Find me something solid, and I'm all in."

Sam set his crumpled beer can on the edge of Kevin's desk and rose to his feet. "Guess I'm going on a road trip. What's the name of this town?"

"Minnow Bay."

"Okay." *My stuff is still packed. I need to check my supplies—*

"Before you head out, tell me about the businesses being targeted in Regency Bay."

"Maisie?" He paused with his hand on the doorknob.

"These are small businesses, right? Family owned? And some of them are in historic buildings?"

He nodded.

A wide grin spread over her features. "I can help them. It's what I do. If there are any grants these people qualify for, I'll find them."

"And if they have enough funding to secure their property—"

Kevin's grin was positively wolfish. "It won't matter if I can't find anything to charge this guy with, if these people aren't vulnerable to buyout."

Sam glanced from Kevin to Maisie with a grin of his own—the first since this whole mess began. "I see why you married her."

Kevin winked at him. "Maybe you'll be as lucky someday."

Chapter Eighteen

Tuesday morning Sophie sipped at what used to be iced coffee, but was now just a tepid mess. She drank it anyway. *At least the caffeine should kill this damn headache.* "How's next weekend looking?"

Wilf leafed through the sheaf of files in his hands. "The guest speaker from Oregon is scheduled to arrive Thursday evening. We have six sets of kids booked to wear the Oliver and Octavia costumes—"

"Six *sets?*"

Wilf shrugged. "Can't have Otter Fest without the otters and those suits get hot, especially on a bright summer day."

"Point taken."

"We've got the materials for the kids craft stations, and the high school science club will be acting as ecology ambassadors. Everything is in tents on the boardwalk, so the event won't be hindered by the situation at the Longbourn."

"Unless we have weather."

"In which case, we'll move to the high school gymnasium."

She squinted at her notepad. "And all the special Otter Fest merch arrived?"

"Received and on display as we speak. Everything is set for the grand opening Friday."

"Good. Anything else?" She winced at the sound of

her own voice.

He peered at her over the top of his glasses, worry etched on his face. "One more thing. Several business owners have received emails from a lawyer named Margaret Curtis, representing something called the Small Business Heritage Foundation."

What fresh hell is this? She shook her head, which worsened the pounding in her temples. "Do we know anything about this organization? Is it legit?"

"I'm about to do some digging. It looks…promising."

"How so?"

"According to their website, the foundation aids small, family-owned businesses, particularly those that are multi-generational or occupy vintage buildings. They help clients find grants and programs for bringing their technology up to date or preserving their premises."

"It sounds…"

"Too good to be true?"

Sophie sighed. "I was gonna say, like exactly what we need, but yeah. That, too."

"Hence my digging. Go eat and take something for your headache."

Sophie didn't move from her chair. "How's the situation at the Longbourn?"

Wilf huffed, but consulted his notes. "Every business in town that can, has offered help or discounts, but it's really beyond patching and repairs. They'll need to replace the entire electrical system in the very near future. Ned has contractors coming this week for estimates." He peered at her over the tops of his glasses. "We were extraordinarily lucky the power simply failed. If there had been a fire—"

"We could have lost a significant portion of the boardwalk." She shuddered. "Great. Now we're into public safety. There's only so long before the fire marshal has to step in and do a full inspection…" She sucked in a deep breath. "Okay. I need you to set up a meeting with the management of all four hotels. The boarding houses, too, and anyone else you think could be helpful. Tell them to bring notes about their projected occupancy and whatever events they have scheduled for the rest of the summer. We're going to sit down and figure out how to redistribute everything around the Longbourn's repairs."

The door banged open, admitting Bonnie. She waved a familiar battered phone case. "Hey Soph—look what turned up in the lost and found from the party." She dropped it in Sophie's outstretched hand. "Battery's dead, but it doesn't look like anyone stepped on it or dropped it in the punch bowl."

"Small blessings."

"Hey—we'll take what we can get."

Wilf snatched the phone and plugged it into the charger on his desk. "You can go take care of that headache while it's charging. I'll start making calls."

Sophie hauled herself to her feet. "Remind me again which one of us is in charge here?"

Bonnie smirked and pointed unerringly at Wilf.

****

Sam almost missed the turn off for Minnow Bay. The old-fashioned wooden sign listed to one side and was badly in need of repainting. An out of service neon sign missing most of its letters overshadowed it. A frown settled on his face as he cruised down the main drag. Windows of vacant buildings stared balefully out over streets lined with beat up older vehicles. Garbage overflowed corner trash cans and skittered along the curb. It looked more like an inner city than a quaint seaside village.

At the end of the street, acres of empty asphalt parking lot surrounded soulless concrete buildings blocking the view of the bay. Weeds sprouted from cracks in the pavement and shards of broken glass glittered in the sun. *This is what they want to do to Regency Bay.*

A muscle ticked in his jaw as he pulled into a parking space in front of the municipal building. *Not if I have anything to say about it.* He grabbed his camera bag from the trunk, then locked the car. He pulled out his camera and started taking pictures. He recorded all of it—the graffiti, the broken glass, the shuttered businesses. There were no quaint little eateries or antique shops—none of the things you'd expect in a small town. The only places doing any business were fast foods and chain convenience stores. Even the old-fashioned brick bank on the corner had gaudy modern signage screwed into its once-genteel façade.

Sam's guts roiled and he headed toward the concrete monoliths at the end of the street. *If I don't get a breath of fresh air soon—*

A police cruiser pulled up alongside him and the window rolled down. "'Afternoon. Can I help you?"

Sam eyed the officer behind the wheel. The mirrored sunglasses were a necessity this close to the ocean and didn't give away any hints of the man's personality. His nametag read "Sheriff Mitchell."

He lowered the camera. "Maybe. You lived here long?"

The sheriff huffed out a mirthless bark of laughter. "All my life. That long enough?"

"Then maybe you can tell me how all this"—he gestured with his free hand—"happened."

"I could. Hop in. I'll take you to see the bay. Or what's left of it."

This does not sound promising.

****

This is worse than I imagined. I wish to God Sophie didn't have to see this. But she did. They all did, or Minnow Bay's reality could become Regency Bay's future. A rank breeze smelling of dead things blew in from the bay. Most of the beach had eroded, but what sand remained was host to a field of litter. Most of the high-rise resort buildings were steel-shuttered and padlocked. As Kevin told him, two currently housed economy grade chain hotels and another had been converted to a discount retail store. Sam snapped away, shot after shot, ignoring the irritating whiff of smoke from the sheriff's cigarette.

"What can you tell me about the town, before the deal with Darrell Masterson and Seaside Holdings?"

The sheriff scanned the area as he spoke. "How does a roving photographer know about our deal with the devil?"

Sam shrugged slightly, checking his last image. "It's a matter of public record."

"It is indeed." Sheriff Mitchell dropped his cigarette butt on the sidewalk and ground it out under his heel. "Minnow Bay got its name because the kelp beds used to be spawning grounds for all sorts of fish." He pointed at a spot beyond the chain link fence installed to keep people from wandering into the surf. "There used to be a fishing pier out there and a couple of nice catch-of-the-day restaurants. They all dried up—"

"When the otters disappeared?"

"You know your ecology."

"I have smart friends."

"Then I guess you'll understand this next bit. With no otters, the damned sea urchins took over the bay and ate up all the kelp. No kelp, no minnows. No minnows, no fish. We hung on for a while. This used to be a quiet little place people liked to come and get away from it all. The streets were filled with little shops and such that had been in families for generations. But as the water quality deteriorated, tourism dwindled, and folks found it harder to maintain the older buildings." He eyed Sam shrewdly over the tops of his sunglasses. "None of this seems to surprise you."

Sam shook his head. "There's a town a couple hours away from here called Regency Bay."

"Heard about that. They got a real clever mayor who did a lot of work to reclaim the bay."

"She did. But now—"

"Now a lot of those older businesses need refurbishing, and it costs more than a small town brings in in a season. Enter Darrell Masterson."

"Yeah. I'm trying to help. I don't want..." He winced.

"You don't want your town to end up like this one. Fair enough." The sheriff stared out over the bay, obviously seeing the ghosts of things long gone. "What do you intend to do with all those pictures you been taking?"

And this is where the plan goes off the rails. "I'm not positive. Maybe the Regency Bay Clarion? I have to make sure people in the town know what can happen if Masterson and his company get a foothold on the boardwalk."

"This is the worst-case scenario. We're a little too far from major transportation hubs, and a little too cold and damp in winter." He shrugged. "Masterson learned from his mistakes. It might not be so bad for your town."

"Is there anything you can tell me that might help? Did Masterson break any laws? Threaten people?"

The sheriff laughed. "Son, you've been watching too many movies. There were no roving gangs of thugs with baseball bats. Masterson's paperwork was ironclad. Believe me, I've looked. If there was anything any of us could have sued him for, we woulda done it years ago. I'm sorry. I wish I could give you something solid. I'd hate to see this happen to some other town."

"Maybe it's not too late." Sam dug his wallet from his back pocket and fished out a couple of business cards. "This is the research station at Regency Bay. They can advise you about the water quality. This is an organization that might be able to help the remaining small businesses. And this is for the mayor's office. Sophie spearheaded most of the reclamation projects. I know she'd be happy to share her experience."

Sheriff Mitchell chuckled. "Know her that well, do you?"

"I do." *Whatever she might think of me right now, I know she'll help these people if she can.*

Chapter Nineteen

Sophie sat at her desk, staring at her phone. She'd sorted through everything in her inbox and email twice. She triple checked that the plans for Otter Fest were on track. She even scheduled herself for a couple of tours. She'd sorted through all the voicemails and texts that accumulated while her phone languished in the depths of the hotel lost and found basket. There was only one left. She let it play.

"Sophie, I really hope you didn't just delete this when you saw my name. I wouldn't blame you, but...I need you to hear this. I resigned. I'm leaving Regency Bay tonight—just for a little while. I hope. I'm going to Sacramento to see my brother. He's in corporate law. My sister-in-law, Maisie, works with small businesses. I'm going to make this right. I have to...so I can come home to Regency Bay...and you. I mean...if you'll still have me. Because Sophie...I'm in love with you."

"Oh, Sam..." She closed her eyes, images dancing through her mind...laughing together in her kitchen...making love on the couch...waking up together with Carb and Ginny curled at the foot of the bed, as if he'd always belonged there... *But I didn't think falling in love was supposed to hurt so much.*

"You're hurting because what you and Sam have together is real."

Her eyes shot open, staring at Wilf in the doorway.

149

"Did I…?"

"No. You didn't say it out loud. You didn't have to. I've known you all your life." He made a show of sorting through the folders in her in box. "You care deeply. It's what makes your friendship—and your love—such a treasure. Have you heard from him?"

She gestured to her phone. "Voicemail, while my phone was MIA. He went to see his brother, who's in corporate law. Sam thought he might have some ideas if Northanger Holdings is breaking any regulations. And his sister-in-law Maisie works with small businesses."

Wilf paused. "Maisie is short for Margaret. Those emails—"

"Are from her." A smile tugged at the corners of Sophie's mouth as she searched for a contact on her phone.

"I'll leave you to it." Wilf pulled the office door shut with a quiet click.

****

Sophie banged her fist on the table to no avail. Arguments raged around the conference room, reigniting the headache she'd been fighting since this whole mess began. *Maybe if I barf on the table they'll shut up?*

"Can't sell—"

"Split the boardwalk—"

"—give in to this guy!"

Fweeeeeeeeet!

She winced and turned to the doorway.

Bonnie winked, then removed the whistle from her mouth. "Awright. All of you sit down and shut up. The next one who speaks out of turn gets a citation."

"But—"

Bonnie smirked and pulled out her ticket book.

The offender subsided back into their chair.

Sophie scrubbed her hands over her face, then straightened in her seat.

A thin, balding man wearing a pinstriped shirt and bowtie timidly raised his hand.

"Yes, Ned?"

He glanced nervously around the room. "Look, I don't want to sell. I don't think I have a choice anymore. We've all known this would happen sooner or later. Spot repairs only work for so long. Renovations on such an old building costs plenty. I had to take out a loan to cover the new boiler last winter. I'm running out of options."

"Can the work be done piecemeal? So you don't have to shut down entirely?"

Ned shuffled through a sheaf of papers. "I suppose so. But I don't see how it helps. We have to start in the ballroom—that's where the circuit failed. It'll take time. Those antique chandeliers have to be rewired and then rehung and it's delicate work. It can't be rushed. Once I lose the revenue from the reenactors' ball...well, I don't see how I can afford to make the repairs and stay in business. I have bills, payroll, insurance...and it's all going to snowball from there. I'll have to rewire the kitchen and then all the guest rooms—"

Murmurs raced around the table. Bonnie licked a finger and opened her ticket book, then pulled a pen from behind her ear and clicked it, poised to start writing. Silence ensued.

Sophie raised a hand. "Okay. One thing at a time. We're okay for this weekend?"

Wilf nodded. "Most of the Otter Fest events take place outside or at the research center. We have a bit of breathing space."

"Good. Now, where can we move the reenactors' ball? It's not as insanely crowded as the cosplayers' event."

Wilf nodded. "The party at Pride and Promises is drawing off some of the crowd. This event uses acoustic instruments, so we don't need an elaborate sound system." He glanced around the table. "Marge?"

"I'm sorry, but I'm catering the banquet."

"Charlie? What about the Netherfield?"

The assistant manager shrugged apologetically. "We've got the vendors in our event space."

Sophie glanced at the empty chair meant for manager of the Norland.

"Jake's dealing with a plumbing issue," Wilf told her. "And the speakers and workshops are in the Norland's conference rooms."

Great. Plumbing. The next disaster waiting to happen. "Could we move them? Or the vendors?" Sophie suggested. "What about the high school gym?"

Marge wrinkled her nose. "It's not terribly attractive for a history event."

"And what about my contracts?" Charlie demanded. "I'm set up and staffed for vendors, not a big party."

Fweeeeeeeeet!

The whistle cut through Sophie's head like a knife, but served its purpose. "Folks! This isn't about any one of you—it's about all of us. Together. If Northanger gets their claws into the Longbourn, it splits the boardwalk in half. How long can the rest of you hold out if that happens? We need to work together to make it through the rest of this season."

Wilf glanced around the table. "Ahem. What if we leave the vendors at the Netherfield and use the

Assembly Room at the library for the dance? It's a much more pleasant setting than the gym."

Approving murmurs and nods ran around the table.

Ned looked around before raising his hand again. "How will we get people there?"

A fellow in the corner raised a hand. "How about horse and carriage?"

"And how much is that gonna cost?" someone shouted.

He shrugged. "I'll do it for free, in exchange for some promotional consideration."

"Come see me afterward," Wilf told him, with an approving smile.

Sophie slumped in her seat. "All right. Now, worst case scenario—if we need to relocate guests. Who has vacant rooms next weekend?"

****

Sam cruised down the main drag, looking for a parking spot. As Sheriff Mitchell said, this town wasn't quite so terrible. Bustling chain restaurants and retail stores lined the wide boulevard, culminating in a high-rise resort and spa. Beyond the main street rose anonymous concrete apartment blocks. It seemed neat and prosperous enough, but it had no soul. Each prefab building was a cookie-cutter replica found in any city on the map. None of the charm a quaint coastal town should have. It was as if the town had its heart carved out.

He slid into a parking spot and glanced at his phone. Nothing. Sophie took her job as mayor very seriously. She was on call 24/7 and never without her phone. Which meant by now she'd seen his message and either listened to it or discarded it.

He shoved the phone in his bag and climbed out of

the car, stretching. *I can start wandering and taking pictures or try and find someone I can talk to.* None of the brand name establishments seemed particularly inviting. He shrugged and headed for the coffee shop. *I never met a barista who wasn't chatty.* Instead of the worn brass bell of the Anchor, a synthesized doorbell tone announced his entry. The shop was quiet, except for a scattering of customers seated on tall stools at the tiny round tables hunched over assorted devices. *Must be the lull between breakfast and lunch. This doesn't look like the sort of place that tolerates a leisurely tempo.* He scanned the overpriced selections on the menu board as he approached the counter.

An older woman wearing a uniform ballcap crammed over her gray hair smiled, wiping her hands on her matching apron. Her shiny company name tag read "Millie." "What can I get for you, dear?"

"A small coffee with a shot of vanilla syrup, please."

"Of course." She tapped at her computer screen. "That'll be seven fifty."

He winced and handed over his card.

Millie prepared his drink and slid it across the counter. "Anything else for you today, dearie?"

He took a sip of his steaming-hot coffee. "I wondered if I could talk to someone who could tell me about the town before the resort was built?"

"Well, I've lived here all my life. What did you want to know?"

"What was it like here, before?"

Glancing over her shoulder at the camera trained on her work area, Millie grabbed a towel and spray bottle and wiped down the counter. "Willow Beach was a typical small town. Lots of small family-owned businesses that had been here for generations. This whole street used to be old brick storefronts."

"The kind with cute striped awnings?" He leaned on the counter, apparently perusing the baked goods case.

"Just so. One of them was a little bake shop my grandparents opened when they got married. By the time I inherited it, business had shifted more toward a coffee shop. Maybe a bit like this, but..."

"With some actual heart and soul to it?"

She nodded.

"Honestly, it sounds way more appealing than all this chrome and plastic."

"I suppose it was."

"Look...the company that built this is trying to buy out another town. A town I've grown very fond of. I'm looking for something—anything—I can use to help them."

"Well, I suppose it depends on how much that town wants to be helped." She sighed and folded her towel, rubbing at the glass with the clean side. "You see, owning your own business is wonderful when the weather's great and everything works. But it gets to be a lot, being the one responsible for everything. All it takes is one slow season or one bad storm. Then you find out exactly how old your shop is...and what the going rate is to bring the electric up to code." She favored him with a crooked little smile. "Sound familiar?"

He nodded and took a slurp of his coffee.

"People get tired. When you've been scraping along, two steps ahead of the bill collectors and safety inspectors for years, you just plain get worn out. Then a company comes along and promises to revitalize the whole town and create lots of new jobs? Selling out suddenly seems like a real good idea."

"Did the company come through? With the jobs, I mean?"

"Well, there's plenty of jobs, after a fashion. You need at least two, because none of them are full time. They won't hire locals for management positions. They claim you need a four-year degree for those. Problem is—"

"None of these jobs pay enough to afford tuition?"

"Just so."

"What if I could put you in touch with an agency that helps small businesses?"

She chuckled, putting the cleaner and towel away under the counter. "I don't think there's any left in town. What you see is what you get. It's not the legacy I wanted to leave behind. I don't have any kids of my own, but I'd hoped someday to sell my shop to some young person, who'd give it new life, but...it wasn't meant to be. At least this pays the bills."

"Thanks for your time." He tucked a ten in the tip jar. "Can I have another coffee to go?"

"Sure thing."

Bzzt.

Sam reached for his phone before realizing his bag hadn't vibrated...and another guest was answering a call. *It's been four days. If she wanted to talk to you, you'd know it.*

****

While this town wasn't as overtly distressing as Minnow Bay, it had its own issues...and the idea of Regency Bay, with its quirky cast of characters and eclectic businesses being paved over to make room for this brand of prepackaged "success" made his stomach churn. Not many people were willing to talk to him, but he'd had some luck in the research room at the local library.

Bzzt. Bzzt.

Wait—this time it *was* his bag buzzing. He hastily slung his camera strap over his shoulder and rummaged out his phone. His shoulders slumped with relief when he saw the caller—Sophie. His hands shook as he accepted the call.

"Hi, Sam."

Her voice soothed the knot of tension that had taken up residence in his chest since he left Regency Bay. "Sophie. I...wasn't sure you'd call."

"I'm sorry. There was a sudden power outage at the Longbourn Saturday—"

"What—during the party?" *It must have happened after security booted me out.* "I tried—I wanted to talk to you before I left—"

"Sparrow told me they saw you, but security—"

"Yeah. Not my finest moment."

"Anyway, it was crazy for a while. The emergency lights came on, but evacuating such a large crowd without any kind of public address system was hard. Then once we moved everyone outside, the generators had to be moved in and set up. In the confusion, I dropped my phone. Bonnie just found it yesterday, but the battery died. It's...good to hear your voice."

"Likewise."

"Where are you?"

"A place called Willow Beach."

"That's a dumb name."

"Excuse me—pot, kettle?"

"Okay, I'm not a botanist, but willows don't grow

on the beach!"

"Evidently there's a variety that does well in sandy soil. They're planted all over the place. It's about the only attractive feature of the town. And it might be all that grows here for long, at the rate they're going. The well water isn't good for drinking anymore, so they need bottled water for all the cooking and drinking."

"Too much pressure on the aquifer, so there's saltwater incursion?"

"Um…I guess?"

She chuckled softly. "Underground water sources take time to replenish. When an aquifer is located close to the shore, there needs to be enough fresh water to push the salt water back out to sea. If too much fresh water drains too quickly, the saltwater creeps in."

"In layman's terms?"

"When you use too much water too fast, the wells fill up with seawater."

"Yuck."

"Very yuck. Also very expensive, whether they continue to bring in bottled water or opt to build a water treatment facility."

"I don't think the company behind all this invests too much in infrastructure."

"Yeah."

"And this is one of the better places. I…Sophie, I wish you didn't have to see the one that failed, but people need to know what might happen."

"Are you coming back to town? I could organize a press conference—"

"No! I mean…I think it needs to come from another source. I was thinking the Clarion, maybe. Or the local cable news channel. Something so it looks more impartial…and so everyone sees it at once."

"Why are you doing this?"

"I told you. I need to make this right. I messed up and I need to fix things." He paused. "Do you trust me?"

"Yes." A beat of deep, dark, silence grew and thickened. Then: "I miss you."

"I miss you, too, Soph." He cradled the phone closer, wishing it was her hand he held.

"Sam?"

"Yeah?"

"I…did you mean what you said?"

"Every word." He swore he could hear her blushing.

"Good. Because I'm pretty sure I'm in love with you, too."

Chapter Twenty

Sophie perched on the corner of Wilf's desk, sipping her coffee. "So, it looks like this year's Otter Fest was a resounding success." Sam would have adored it.

"I'd say so, yes. The speaker from Oregon had a full house for both talks. There was only one mascot-related heat injury."

"Good." He would have gotten amazing shots of them playing with the kids. "And you were right. As usual. Six sets of Oliver and Octavia it is. At least for the summer events."

"I'll need you to sign the science club kids' community service certificates."

"With pleasure." He'd have loved seeing all those eager kids and capturing everything on film.

"It looks like we sold through most of the dated merchandise—"

"And whatever's left will probably go for Kids Fest."

Wilf checked his notes. "Without a big formal evening event drawing the majority of the traffic, a lot of restaurants made good numbers. We got through without any major issues at any of the hotels."

"Does it look like we're good for rooms next weekend?"

"We're booked close to capacity right now, but those chain motels out on the thruway—"

"The ones owned by Northanger?"

He nodded grimly. "They're offering cut rates through Labor Day, trying to draw off our guests."

"Well, I don't imagine there's too much we can do about it. But I think the history folks would rather stay in town, even if we have to shift some of them to one of the boarding houses."

"I suspect you're right. However…"

"What? What else?"

"Ned went to the bank to talk about taking out a mortgage on the Longbourn to cover the cost of the electrical repairs. The manager advised him to hold off. It seems there's a company sniffing around, looking to buy up loans and mortgages."

" 'A company.' You mean Northanger." Sophie sank her head into her hands.

"Not openly, but the timing is suspicious. Apparently, this is what Darrell Masterson resorts to when he doesn't get his way."

"Is that legal?"

"I don't know. Corporate finance isn't my forte. Perhaps Sam's brother might have some insight."

"What about the donation buckets from last weekend? Will they help?"

"Perhaps. And I understand the Small Business Heritage Foundation has started grant paperwork for the Longbourn."

She smiled into her coffee cup. *Blessings on Sam's sister-in-law.* "Talk to Ned and see if he can hold on long enough for them to find something."

"Of course."

"What's the schedule for the reenactors to arrive?"

Wilf consulted his calendar. "Vendors should start

arriving Thursday to set up. The rest of the mob scene descends Friday."

"Please remind whoever needs reminding that fire safety trumps historical accuracy."

"So, no candles."

"No candles," she agreed. "No lanterns. No open flames of any kind."

He jotted down a note to himself. "Have you decided what you're going to do about the ball?"

"No, I—"

The door slammed open, revealing Darrell Masterson, clutching a newspaper in his fist. "What's the meaning of this, Ms. Bennet?"

Sophie flipped her braid back over her shoulder. "It's Mayor Bennet, and I have no idea what you're talking about."

He strode forward and slapped the paper down on Wilf's desk, knocking over the pencil cup and scattering its contents over the desk and floor. It was a copy of the day's Clarion, featuring a case study of a nearby town. A color shot of a cracked asphalt parking lot littered with broken glass stared forlornly from the front page.

Wilf glanced at it as he gathered his pens and pencils. "The Clarion is an independent publication. Their editors are free to write about anything they think might interest their readership."

"Don't tell me your boyfriend isn't behind this."

"Excuse me?" Sophie hopped down from the desk.

"These photographs are credited to Sam Trowbridge, whom I terminated—"

"Who resigned, once he discovered who he was really working for."

Masterson waved his hand irritably. "This is an

attempt by a former employee to discredit me and my company and there will be repercussions."

"I believe this is called free press, Mr. Masterson," Wilf replied. "The First Amendment. Perhaps you've heard of it."

"We'll see about that. Something people who quote the First Amendment conveniently tend to forget is that freedom of speech doesn't equal freedom from consequences. Should I find there are any irregularities, such as company employees speaking to a reporter on company time, there will be consequences. For instance, these are photographs of private property—"

Sophie grabbed the paper and skimmed the front page. "The angle looks like these were taken from the public street." She folded the paper and smoothed it carefully. "Tell me, Mr. Masterson, what are you afraid of? If everything Northanger Holdings has planned is completely legal and aboveboard, why should it bother you if people learn the truth about other towns where you've done business?" She glanced at the paper again. "Although, this article is about a failed resort owned by a company called Seaside Holdings. I can't imagine why you think it concerns you."

"Gotta guilty conscience?" Bonnie added, smirking.

Masterson smoothed his tie and adjusted his jacket. "Fine. Enjoy your little victory. I know how much total rewiring of a building the size of the Longbourn costs. I can afford to be patient. Can the owners of the Longbourn? Can you?" He stormed out, trailing a waft of over-priced cologne.

"Don't let the door hit ya," Bonnie muttered, waving a file folder to clear the air. She turned to Sophie with a shit-eating grin. "Anything you wanna share?"

Sophie drained her coffee cup. "Such as?"

"Such as 'boyfriend'?"

"Such as you don't seem entirely surprised by this development," Wilf added.

"I knew something might happen, but not exactly what, when, or how. He—Sam—thought it was better if I didn't know the details."

"Plausible deniability. I like it."

Sophie rolled her eyes. "He thought the information should come from an outside source and be disseminated by the press."

Wilf frowned and folded his arms. "And does this...investigation...involve any trespassing or other questionable activity?"

"Don't answer that," Bonnie said sharply.

Wilf opened his mouth and Bonnie whirled and jabbed a finger at him.

"And you, stop asking incriminating questions."

"But—"

"La lala la lalala," Bonnie sang loudly and off key.

Sophie clapped her hands over her ears. "Okay, okay! Stop with the torture already."

"Repeat after me: plausible deniability."

Sophie glared at her.

"La lala—"

"Fine. Plausible deniability. Happy?"

"Yes. Now go shut yourself in your office and find something to revise for the sixteenth time. I'm sure something needs doing for next weekend. Like figuring out what you're going to wear to the ball and who you're going with." She turned to Wilf. "And you, practice saying 'No comment' with a straight face." She glanced at Sophie. "Hey—when you talk to the hottie, tell him I'm sorry I doubted him."

"When I talk to who?"

Bonnie just grinned and winked.

****

Wednesday afternoon, Sam was settled back in Kevin and Maisie's house, watching developments from afar. The Clarion had broken the Minnow Bay story Monday, with a front page headline, followed by a second article about Willow Beach Tuesday. Today, the local cable news station had picked up both stories.

Staying away was the right thing. He knew it. Still, it was all he could do to keep from jumping in his car and breaking multiple speed limits driving back to Regency Bay—and Sophie. He missed her so much.

Kevin reminded him several times that it was better for the media to present his findings—for him to distance himself, so Sophie could truthfully say she wasn't involved. He also knew Bonnie and Wilf, and Sparrow, and her parents, and hell—the whole town—would make sure she ate and hydrated and looked after herself.

But I'd still rather be there. Marcus'll try to make personal insinuations—he always does. She hates that. I want to hold her hand through this. I want to hold her.

He brought up the Regency Bay local cable channel on his laptop. Yup—there it was—a live press conference starting now. He clicked on the box and a familiar image of the boardwalk resolved.

"Maximize that, would you?" Maisie asked, leaning in as close as Junior's bulk allowed.

"And turn up the volume," Kevin added, hanging over the back of the couch.

He did and Sophie's face filled the screen. She stood

at a podium set up in front of the bandstand. The breeze off the bay ruffled her sleeveless green dress and whipped a couple strands of long ginger hair across her face. His fingers itched to tuck them behind her ear.

Maisie squeezed his arm. "She's lovely."

"Well of course she is," Kevin said. "We Trowbridge brothers have excellent taste in women."

She whapped him with a throw pillow. "And so much humility."

Sam cranked the volume again as he saw Sophie's lips moving.

"—no connection at all. A concerned individual began making inquiries into real estate deals similar to the one proposed for Regency Bay. Local media outlets considered his findings worthy of further investigation."

"A concerned individual who's sleeping with you," a voice Sam recognized as Marcus shouted.

Maisie grabbed her business card file from the coffee table and rifled through it. "Here." She shoved a card at him. "My friend Jane specializes in slander and libel cases. She'd love to take this guy down a peg."

"Shh," Kevin hissed.

"—not a local resident and my personal life isn't the topic of this press conference." Sophie pointed at another reporter. "Yes?"

"What can you tell us about the Small Business Heritage Foundation?"

"The foundation is a private organization that helps small family-owned businesses find grants and government programs to help them navigate today's business environment."

"And how did you find them?"

"They found us. The foundation contacted several

area businesses."

"To help them find legal loopholes to avoid foreclosure and code violations!" Marcus interjected.

Sophie leaned closer to her mic. "To help them take advantage of programs and assistance they might not otherwise be aware of."

Another reporter raised their hand. "And these programs would enable business owners to update their premises and technology?"

"That's the idea."

"But what about all the mudslinging going on around here?" Marcus interrupted, chewing on his unlit cigar.

"Marcus, I'd like to point out every other reporter here is raising their hand to be called on, giving others their respectful attention, not commenting on anyone's private life, or making wild speculations."

He made a show of raising his hand amidst a chorus of guffaws.

Sophie sighed and pointed at him.

"Is she okay?" Maisie whispered. "She looks pale."

She did. A muscle jumped in Sam's jaw. "Sophie doesn't like this sort of thing. She's a very private person."

"And this guy's an ass."

"You have *no* idea."

"What do you have to say to allegations your boyfriend's investigation is a plot to slander the good name of Darrell Masterson, the representative of Northanger Holdings?"

"Again, I'm going to state this investigation is the endeavor of a private individual. And if Mr. Masterson's intentions for Regency Bay are good, then he should have no issue with anyone looking into his previous projects."

A reporter wearing the logo of a large metropolitan newspaper raised his hand. "Mayor Bennet, is it true state environmental officials are planning an investigation into the Willow Beach resort as a result of this story?"

"I can't comment on what state agencies might or might not do."

"Good girl," Kevin muttered.

"Of course." He glanced at his notes. "But I understand your background is in environmental conservation, and you spearheaded the reclamation of Regency Bay. What can you tell us about what officials might find in Willow Beach?"

"Speaking hypothetically, because I've never been to Willow Beach, I can tell you seaside communities like Regency Bay occupy a fragile environment. Nature is meant to exist in balance. When you remove a keystone species, or use too much water, or produce too much waste, the balance suffers. This is why a major development project, such as a resort, requires very careful consideration, to ensure it's the best choice for the community." Her shoulders dropped and color bloomed in her cheeks.

Sam relaxed, too. "She's always better when she can talk about science. It's her passion."

"As the failed Minnow Bay project proves?" the reporter asked.

"No comment."

"Of course. Thank you, Mayor Bennet."

"No comment?" Marcus butted in yet again. "What kind of answer is that?"

"The only one you're getting from me. People need to examine the media coverage and read the facts and decide for themselves."

"And what do you say to the fact an elderly barista who talked to your boyfriend lost her job over this?"

The bottom dropped out of his stomach. "Millie. That damn camera. She was fired for talking to me."

Onscreen, the color Sophie had regained drained from her cheeks so swiftly Sam reached out, as if he could support her through the internet connection. Maisie gripped his hand.

"She can come here. I'll hire her," someone called out from the crowd gathered on the boardwalk.

"Me, too!"

"There's a nice apartment open on my block!"

Others chimed in various offers to help her pack and move her stuff in their trucks or vans.

A small smile played over Sophie's lips. "Well, I guess you have your answer, Marcus."

Kevin thumped his shoulder. "I can see why you like her."

"I want to meet her," Maisie added.

"You'll love her."

She leaned over and kissed his cheek. "I know I will."

Chapter Twenty-One

Friday afternoon Sophie looked up from her computer as Bonnie bounced into her office, shutting the door and muting the constant bustle of the front lobby. "What now?"

Bonnie deposited a bottle of iced tea and a takeout bag from the diner in front of her. "Lunch. So you don't keel over."

"Is it lunchtime?"

"It was. Two hours ago. So eat." Bonnie flopped into one of the guest chairs, obviously not going anywhere until she could truthfully report back to Wilf that Sophie had indeed ingested some food.

Sophie sighed and checked the time. *Dammit, she's right.* She reached for the bag.

"So, what are you wearing tomorrow night?"

Sophie didn't comment, pulling her favorite sandwich—turkey on sourdough with no dead leaves, thank you very much—from the rustling brown paper bag.

"Are you going to reclaim your blue gown from Sparrow? You totally should."

"Bonnie, I love you, but I have a little bit more on my mind right now than what I'm wearing to a party I plan on attending for fifteen minutes, tops." Suddenly ravenous, she scarfed down a big bite of her sandwich and reached for the iced tea.

"Chew and swallow, wouldja? I don't wanna have to remember how to do the Heimlich."

Sophie rolled her eyes, patting her mouth with a paper napkin. "Anyway, this is the history people. My old dress is more historically correct."

"Who cares? Someone will find something to whine about no matter what you wear. Those people are uppity about costumes." Bonnie waggled her fingers, making air quotes.

"Are you gonna wear the lime green monstrosity? They'll really have something to talk about."

"Yup. To the party at Pride and Promises."

"Well, some of us don't have that option." She got in a couple more bites and realized all she could hear was the sound of her own chewing. Bonnie curled in her chair uncharacteristically silent. She gulped down the food in her mouth. What fresh hell was about to descend? "Bonnie? You okay?"

Bonnie looked up and huffed a frizzy curl out of her face. "I really am sorry I didn't have more faith in Sam. He's a good guy."

"Yeah. He is."

"He didn't have to do all that research and visit those towns, but he did it anyway." Bonnie leaned forward on the edge of her chair. "So?"

"So what?"

"So what are you going to do about this—him?"

Sophie poked around under the pile of chips for her pickle spear. "In case you hadn't noticed, we've got all sorts of news media milling around the lobby, an angry real estate developer looking for revenge, and two full weeks left of the high season. I really don't have time—"

"You should make time," Bonnie blurted, cheeks flushing scarlet. "You—he—Sam is perfect for you. You can't let him slip away."

Sophie set the half sandwich she'd been about to take a bite out of back in the box. "You're whistling a new tune. Whatever happened to 'a few weeks of fun between consenting adults'?"

Bonnie's cheeks blazed scarlet. "It has been fun. And…I don't want it to end."

Wow. Ooooookay. "Have you told Finn?"

Bonnie shook her head. "I'm not sure how. I never did…this…before. And it's not like he can stay, even if he wanted to. He's got a position at a prestigious oceanographic research center back East. This was a fellowship or something. Just for the summer. He has to go back and write papers and do science…stuff."

Oh…this is so much worse than the annual post-Labor Day margarita marathon. And it's not like I have any meaningful words of wisdom…or moral high ground…"You still have a couple of weeks together. Maybe concentrate on enjoying the time you've got left."

"Maybe. I mean, there are still a couple places we haven't—"

"Bonnie!"

Bonnie smirked unrepentantly for a moment, then her expression dimmed again.

"You know, I get Finn has the sort of job he can't walk away from, but you don't."

"Gee, thanks for the reminder of my mediocrity."

"I didn't mean it like that, and you know it. You're woven into the heart of this town, and I'd miss the hell out of you. But realistically, in a town this size, in such a small police department, when's the next time a promotion will open up? Ten years? Twelve?"

Bonnie slunk down in her chair, arms crossed.

"So even if you wanted to make a career in law enforcement a priority, you'd have to leave here to do it. And we both know you're not the sort of person whose life revolves around your job. You could go with him."

Bonnie shot her a look. "We also both know I'm not the sort of girl you bring home to grandma."

"Hey! Don't talk about my best friend that way!"

Bonnie twisted her hands in her lap, picking at her nail polish. "Even if he wanted to bring his summer fling home with him, what am I gonna do in Massachusetts?"

"You'd be living in a seaside community, same as here. There's gotta be a boardwalk that wants patrolling."

"Massachusetts. They've got winter there."

"We've got winter here."

"Not with, like, feet of snow! I'd have to wear a coat and boots and stuff." She shuddered.

Sophie shrugged. "Could be fun. And you'd have Finn to keep you warm. And guess what? They've got fall there—proper fall with colored leaves and pumpkins and cornstalks—and you'd be within driving distance of Salem. You'd love it there."

Bonnie shook her head, but at least she was grinning—or trying to. It looked a bit forced to Sophie's expert eye.

"What about you?"

"How do you mean?"

"Well, Sacramento isn't so far away. I mean, at least it's in the same state. You could still see each other. It's totally not the same thing as Jerk Number One and Jerk Number Two."

"I know."

"You could really make it work this time."

"I know."

"Sophie!"

"I know I—we—could really make it work this time." Her lip curled in a smirky little smile. "Especially since Sam wants to relocate to Regency Bay."

Bonnie flung herself across the desk, engulfing Sophie in a bear hug. "Wah-*hoo!* You *go* girl!"

Sophie winced, hugging Bonnie with one arm and attempting to hold her bottle of iced tea out of harm's way with the other hand. "They probably heard you all the way out on the boardwalk," she grumbled.

"We certainly heard her in the lobby," Wilf called through the closed door.

****

Sam sat at the island in Maisie's kitchen, picking at his share of Junior's post-lunch-pre-dinner snack.

Maisie bumped his shoulder. "Hey. Why so glum? You did it."

"Yeah." He dragged his spoon through his mac and cheese, not scooping any up.

"Sam." She was practicing her Mom voice, and it worked.

He laid down his spoon and turned to face her.

"You got major news outlets to break a huge story. The environmental people are opening an investigation into Willow Beach, and the foundation is finding grants and programs for businesses in Regency Bay. We even started the paperwork for a historical listing for the boardwalk. You did a good thing."

"But I screwed up. I worked for bad people."

"And you quit, as soon as you became aware of it."

"I hurt people I care about. I hurt Sophie. And I got Millie fired for talking to me. Darrell Masterson was very gleeful about it."

"And that stinks, but you saw what happened at the press conference—she has a ton of offers waiting for her in Regency Bay. Jobs, apartments, even help moving and packing."

"But she's older and now she has to uproot her whole life because I had to go and poke my nose into things."

She sighed and rubbed his arm. "I know, but from what you told me, there isn't much left of the place she grew up in. I think one she's settled, she'll find Regency Bay is a lot closer to the sort of small-town ambience she's used to."

"Maybe. I hope so."

"So, when are you leaving?"

"Booting me out already?"

"Never. But you've got someone waiting for you. And I understand there's a ball tomorrow night."

"This one is the reenactor's ball. It's strictly historically documented dances set to strictly documented music played on extant or reproduction instruments. I understand they're fussier about the costumes, too."

"That…sounds a bit dry. Interesting, but dry."

He shrugged one shoulder. "The others are more hybrid—some English country dances mixed with regular music."

Her eyes sparkled. "I've never been to a ball. You'll have to bring us to one when we come visit you."

He snorted. "Good luck stuffing Kevin into those stupid breeches."

"Who knows? He might like it. You did."

"I had a certain motivation."

"Named Sophie. And she's waiting for you." she nudged his arm. "Now go get her."

Chapter Twenty-Two

"Quit squirming," Bonnie scolded.

"Quit fussing," Sophie replied. "I'm staying at this thing fifteen minutes, tops. One dance and I'm out of there."

"Doesn't mean your night ends there." Bonnie added a few more hairpins, seeming to poke them straight into Sophie's skull.

"Oh, yes it does."

"Why? You could make an appearance at the convention, then stop by the fun party. I mean, you should, in the interest of equity."

"One party a night is more than enough for me. Besides, you'll be having enough fun for both of us."

"Well, yeah. But what if the hottie shows up? Don't you want to look breathtakingly gorgeous for him?"

"Stop calling him that. Why would you think he'd turn up tonight? And we both know I'm not the breathtakingly gorgeous type."

Bonnie pinned the circlet of flowers in place with more care than she'd shown for Sophie's scalp. "Soph, you wear this stuff like you escaped from one of those fancy British movies."

"That's what Sam said." *Oops. I shouldn't have repeated that.*

Bonnie smirked. "So, if he comes, you'll want to look gorgeous for him."

"And if he doesn't?"

"Then we'll take lots of pictures, so he knows what he's missing." She glanced at the dark blue silk gown hanging on the back of Sophie's office door. "You know, I bet Sparrow still has the other dress."

"I'm sure they sold it. It's too pretty to linger on the rack and they've had tons of brides through their shop."

"Always assuming they put it back on the rack."

"I hope they did. I wouldn't want them losing a sale."

"You know, Sparrow is a grown person, and if they think having the mayor modeling one of their dresses is a better investment than a random sale, I'd say it's their business." Bonnie came around the chair and took Sophie's hands in hers. "You worry so much about other people, you forget you're important, too. You are!" She squeezed Sophie's hands. "You deserve to be happy and loved and have a kick-ass new dress and live happily ever after with the hottie."

Sophie extricated her hands and engulfed her friend in a hug. "So do you." She pulled back half a step. "Have you talked to Finn?"

Bonnie looked down. "I told you…I don't know how to do this serious stuff. I'm summer fun girl, remember?"

"Just…tell him how you feel."

"And what if he…I dunno…laughs or something?"

"If he laughs, we'll put itching powder in his wetsuit."

"Sophie!"

"But I don't think he will." She grabbed Bonnie's blinding green satin dress from the coat rack and slipped it off the hanger. "Come on—put this thing on so I can button you up." She guided the dress over Bonnie's head, mindful of her fancy updo. "Are you going to keep it?"

"Maybe. Haven't decided yet."

Sophie fastened the row of tiny buttons on the back. "It really suits you. And you've given Phoebe's so much good advertising, they should make you a great deal."

"But if I move to Massachusetts, where would I wear it?" Bonnie smoothed down the rustling satin skirt.

"I told you—you'd be within driving distance of Salem—the Halloween capitol of the world. I'm sure you'll have plenty of—"

There was a diffident tap at the door. "Are you ladies decent?"

"Have you met us?" Bonnie replied.

"What do you need, Wilf?" Sophie called, fastening her earrings with the aid of the small mirror she kept in her desk drawer.

"Sophie, we have a bit of a situation out here."

She glanced down at her shorts and top, then the white knee socks and slippers she'd put on in preparation to changing into her gown. *What the hell. They've seen people running around in half a costume before. It's nothing too strange around here.*

Ned stood out in the lobby, wringing his hands.

"What happened?"

Wilf passed her two notices printed on town stationery, complete with embossed seals.

She skimmed the contents, frowning. "The fire marshal and the building inspector? Both?"

Wilf nodded. "In response to the safety concerns raised by a local citizen."

"Darrell Masterson isn't a citizen."

"Marcus is," Ned spat, two spots of bright red

staining his thin cheeks.

Bonnie appeared in the doorway in all her satin bedecked glory. "Marcus is a—"

"Not helpful," Sophie muttered.

"They're shutting down the Longbourn—right now—Saturday evening in the middle of an event!"

Sophie looked at Wilf. "Can we do anything about this?"

He shook his head. "Not really. There are legitimate safety concerns, and once someone's made an official complaint…" He spread his hands helplessly.

The fire chief let himself into the lobby, removing his uniform cap and tucking it under his arm. "Sophie, I'm so—"

She waved him off. "No—none of this is your fault. You're doing your job. I'd be disappointed in you if you didn't."

He nodded grimly. "And if there's any hint of collusion, Marcus will make damn sure it gets front page coverage in his paper."

Sophie pivoted. "Wilf, get on the phone to the other hotels. Find out if any of them lost any business to those cut-rate deals at the thruway motels. Bonnie, you call the boarding houses. We've already moved the dance, and the vendors are set up at the Netherfield, so it's just guest rooms, right Ned?"

He nodded.

The fire chief cleared his throat. "I've called in all my guys. Just tell me where people are going, and we'll get 'em there." He offered a one-shouldered shrug. "Least I can do."

****

Sam checked his watch as he approached town hall.

If she's already left for the dance, I'll catch up, but I really want to talk to her privately first. I've still got that much self-respect. He dodged out of the way as a uniformed volunteer firefighter trundled a loaded luggage cart down the boardwalk. *What the heck?* He passed through the propped open lobby doors into a scene of barely contained chaos.

"Okay, room three ten is moving to the Delaford," Wilf called without looking up from his computer screen.

"On it," another fireman replied cheerfully, heading out the door.

Sophie had her back to the entrance, talking on her cell phone. Her beautiful red hair was swept up in a circlet of silk flowers and she wore blue satin slippers...along with her shorts and top. She was the loveliest thing he'd ever set eyes on.

She held the phone against her shoulder. "Where can we put a family of five that needs a crib?"

"Barton Cottage has a double," Bonnie replied, resplendent in her green satin gown. The matching headband sat a bit crooked on top of her frizzy curls.

"They can borrow the crib from their current room," a thin man Sam vaguely recognized from one of the hotels added.

No one noticed him yet.

"I can help move them," Finn offered. He wore his costume breeches and an Otter Fest T-shirt.

Sam set down his bags and cleared his throat. "How can I help?"

Sophie whirled. "Sam?" She stood frozen until Wilf gently took the phone from her hand. "What...what are you doing here?"

"There's a ball tonight, isn't there?"

"Sure is," Bonnie said, grinning broadly.

"The Mayor is expected to attend, right?"

Sophie nodded.

"Thought you could use a dance partner. If you'll have me."

He never quite grasped how she closed the distance so quickly and hurled herself into his arms. Well, arm, anyway. He clutched a small green plant embellished with an enormous bow in one hand. His arm locked around her waist, holding her close, while he pressed his lips to the crown of her head.

After a moment, she loosened her death grip on him and craned her neck, trying to see what was tickling her. "What is that?"

Heat creeping up his cheeks, he offered her the small plant. "It's…um…for the last ball, I'd ordered you a nosegay from Foxglove's, but they cancelled my order when everyone thought I was evil. Tonight, I just missed their floral designer, but I wanted to bring you something. So, um…it's catnip."

"Catnip."

"For Carb and Ginny."

"I love it." She set the little plant down on the edge of Wilf's desk and twined both arms around his neck.

"What's going on here?" Everyone had their undivided attention focused on their respective screens, for which he was devoutly grateful.

"The Longbourn was shut down this evening, so we're relocating all the guests to other properties."

"Can I help?" He traced his thumbs over her waist. "I'd really like to help."

"I think you and Sophie need to step into her office

to discuss that very important matter," Wilf suggested.

Bonnie smirked gleefully.

"I…right. The important…thing."

Sophie hesitated.

"Go on," Wilf told her. "We've got this."

"I know you do." She grabbed Sam's hand and towed him into her office, shutting the door with a thump.

****

Sophie turned and leaned her back against the door. "Hey."

"Hey." His lips curled in the crooked little smile she loved so much. "I like your outfit. Doesn't look very historical, though."

She touched her hair self-consciously. "We got a little distracted."

"What is all the commotion?" He waved a hand in the general direction of the lobby.

"The fire chief is ticked he got pulled into this mess, so he asked his guys to help move guests around. When the researchers caught wind of what was happening, a bunch of them offered to double up for the rest of the season, and free up more rooms. Then they came here to help."

"This town is amazing."

"It is, isn't it?"

"Is the ball still happening? 'Cuz I'd really like to take you."

"Yeah, the dance is still on. We'd already moved it to the library."

"Is it okay that I came back?"

She stepped closer, blinking back a sheen of tears. "It's very okay."

"And did it help? The stuff we dug up about those other towns, I mean."

She smoothed her hands over his shoulders, reveling in the solid warmth of him. "Well, it scared Darrell and Marcus into drastic measures, so I guess that's something."

He smiled and settled his hands on her waist. "Will it cause you problems if we're seen together?"

"I don't care." She curled her fingers into the soft cotton of his T-shirt.

"I do." He cradled her face in his palm, stroking his thumb over her cheek. "I don't want to undo all your hard work. If you need me to step back, I can. I mean, I won't like it, but—"

She pushed up on her toes and pressed her lips to his. "I need you right here with me, for this stupid dance and the party after and figuring out how to finish the season when we're short one hotel—"

He leaned down and kissed her. She wound her arms around his neck, pressing close enough to feel the wild galloping of his heart right through both of their shirts. They were both a bit breathless when they broke apart long moments later.

"I want you here for all of it."

Sam leaned his forehead against hers. "Good, because I think they just put a family of five who need a crib in my old room."

"You could stay at my place."

"If you're sure."

Am I? What if people talk? Do I care? No. Not if I've got him. "Very sure. Besides, you need to give Carb and Ginny their present."

"Okay. And we don't have to…I mean…I can camp

out on the couch…"

"Only if I can camp out with you."

Someone cleared their throat rather ostentatiously outside the office door.

"Madame Mayor, might I remind you, you need to make an appearance at the ball, and you're not even dressed yet."

She rolled her eyes. "Okay, Wilf. Send Bonnie in to help me with my gown, would you?"

"Send the hottie out first. I'm not into—"

"Bonnie!"

Chapter Twenty-Three

Sam looked up from his phone as the door to Sophie's office opened. He saw her eyes widen as she noticed the khakis and button down he'd changed into. "Sorry…I returned my costume to Phoebe's when I left town. This is all I had in my bag."

"You look fine."

He stood and stuffed the phone in his pocket. "You look beautiful." *Even more beautiful than I remembered.*

A delightful rosy blush crept up her cheeks.

"I spoke to my brother."

"Yeah?" She fiddled with her tiny purse and fan.

"He says since the major news outlets ran the story, and the environmental people are getting in on the act, his boss gave him the okay to look into Northanger Holdings, as well as Darrell Masterson's past endeavors."

"Which means what, exactly?"

"It means Mr. Masterson will be very occupied with assorted government agencies picking through his files for a while. All his current deals are on hold."

"For how long?" Wilf asked.

"Long enough for Maisie's foundation and the state historical people to find ways to protect the local businesses."

Sophie flung herself into his arms again. He lifted her right off her satin-slippered feet and spun her around.

Wilf took off his glasses and mopped his face with a handkerchief.

"Group hug!" Bonnie yelled, tackling them.

Sam fell back half a step before finding his balance.

Finn slipped his arm around Bonnie, then reached his other arm over her and shook Sam's hand. "I'm sorry I doubted you, mate."

"*I* doubted me, so I can hardly blame you."

"Still, I apologize."

Wilf replaced his glasses, beaming. "I think you all have places to be, don't you?"

"Are you sure you don't want to come with us to the fun party?" Bonnie wheedled.

Sophie smoothed her dress, still keeping one arm wrapped around him. "We need to make an appearance at the convention, but we might stop by Pride and Promises, too." She nibbled her bottom lip and glanced up at him. "If it's okay with you?"

"Anything. Anywhere you want to go."

She stretched up and pressed her lips to his.

"All right, you two," Wilf said, beaming, "go find yourselves a carriage."

"I was gonna say get a room," Bonnie teased, "but a carriage works, too."

Wilf clapped his hands over his ears.

"We can catch one at the Netherfield, right?" Sam asked.

"Yes. They're stopping at all the hotels."

"Don't do anything I wouldn't do!" Bonnie called as she and Finn headed out.

Sophie shook her head.

He offered his arm formally, even though the gesture was at odds with his contemporary clothing.

Sophie linked her arm through his.

"I'm sorry you don't have flowers," he murmured.

"I'm not. Carb and Ginny will love the catnip." She bumped her head against his shoulder. "Why are we walking all the way to the Netherfield?"

"I want to see if Sparrow still has those shoes. At least I'd be sort of correct?"

"Not sure how well 'sort of' works with the history people, but sure. Why not?"

****

"Oh no, hon." Sparrow shook their head, causing the ruffles and ribbons on their cap to quiver. A truly spectacular maroon taffeta gown swept the floor and rustled with their movements. "No way they'll let you in dressed in those clothes."

Sam offered a one-shouldered shrug. "I returned my costume when I left town. This is the best I've got."

"Do you have anything we could buy or rent?" Sophie asked, glancing around the shop.

Sparrow shook their head again, taking a sip from a large paper cup. "I only create bespoke men's clothing. I couldn't loan you someone else's special order even if I had it on hand. And none of my personal pieces would fit you." They poked their head out of their conference room. "Jack, darling, do you have anything in stock that might fit my friend Sam? He's got formal dress pumps and silk stockings."

A ruddy-faced gentleman sporting mutton chop whiskers who looked like he escaped from a Dickens novel waved from a neighboring room. "Send 'im on down, luv."

Sam squeezed her arm before stepping away.

"Which party are you going to?" Sophie asked.

"All of them, darling. I'll take a few turns around the reenactors' ball, then go on to the party at Pride and Promises. Gotta live it up, the last night of my summer season in Regency Bay."

"And you'll be back for the Halloween event?"

"Wouldn't miss it. I'll have orders for some fall and winter brides ready and I'm just as happy not to trust those to delivery services."

Sophie shuddered. *Wedding dresses lost in delivery land? That's a special kind of hell.*

"Hold this while I go look for his shoes, would you?" Sparrow pressed their cup into her hands, then rustled behind a curtain into their storage area. "I hope Jack's got something suitable for a ball in his size. These shoes will look silly with anything working class."

"I'm sure whatever your friend has in stock will be fine."

"Madame Mayor, you can't have lived here all your life and think the reenactors will let him get away with anything less than perfect historical accuracy. Now where did I put his bag?"

More rustling noises and some muttering.

"Excuse me?" Sophie asked, stepping closer to the curtain.

"Found it!" Sparrow erupted from behind the curtain, bag in hand. They blundered right into Sophie, jostling the cup and spilling the contents all over the front of her gown.

"Dammit!"

"Oh, honey, I am so sorry." They reached onto the storage area for a roll of paper towels. "Let me see..." They dabbed at the front of her dress. "It's just water...I don't permit anything else in my shop..."

What else could possibly happen today? "It's fine." She shook out the sodden folds of her skirt.

"Oh, no. The mayor can't appear at a ball like this."

Sophie forced a smile. "It's just water. It'll dry."

Sam appeared, properly dressed in buff breeches and waistcoat, a pristine white shirt, and midnight blue tailcoat, but barefoot, carrying his street clothes over his arm. "What happened here?"

"It's nothing—"

"She can't possibly go to a ball looking like a laundress—"

Sam looked from one to the other. "This doesn't quite add up, folks."

Sophie glanced at him and froze, her jaw dropping a tiny bit. Those breeches clung in *all* the right places, and one lock of hair drooped over his forehead. Her fingers itched to push it back. "You look amazing."

"See? He looks amazing. You look like a drowned rat. I've got the perfect solution." Sparrow bustled behind the curtain again, appearing a moment later holding a familiar blue gown with a white lace overlay, swathed in plastic. "Ta-da!"

"I can't—"

"Sure you can, hon." They winked. "It's yours."

Sam dropped his clothes on a handy chair and took her hands. "Really, Soph. It's yours."

She glanced at Sparrow uncertainly.

They nodded. "Really. He paid for it online."

Sam stroked his thumbs over the backs of her hands. "You said your old dress was full of bad memories. I wanted to make up for the mess I helped create. This is for you—so we can make a whole bunch of new memories. Good ones." He raised her hands and pressed his lips to one, then the other. "Starting tonight."

She laughed through a shimmer of tears. "I like the sound of that."

Sparrow grabbed her arm, tugging her toward the changing booth. "Come on, let's get you changed." They glanced at Sam. "And you, put on those shoes and stockings. We've got parties to get to!"

****

Sophie laughed as Sam swung her down from the carriage.

"You guys weren't joking about the costume police." He kept his hands on her waist, even after her feet were firmly on the boardwalk.

"I think the only reason I got away with this dress is that it's bad form to toss the mayor out after you invite her to your party. But I'm sorry I didn't think of gloves for you. I told you—this isn't really my thing." She smoothed her hands over his chest. "How much did all this set you back?"

"I look on it as an investment in our future."

"If you're sure that's what you want."

"Very." He kissed her forehead. "Having my photos run in multiple big newspapers is great publicity." He clasped her hand in his and strolled toward the lights and music. "Why are there two parties tonight anyway? Just curious."

"The living history people are so particular about clothing and etiquette, so Pride and Promises countered with a 'come as you are' party. In this case, I'm very glad because the assembly room at the library can just about accommodate the living history people without adding this crowd."

Partiers spilled out the double front doors of Pride

and Promises onto the boardwalk. A happy crowd wearing decidedly un-historical costumes boogied and shimmied to contemporary dance tunes.

Sam leaned down and murmured in her ear. "Are you sure you're up for two of these things in one night? We don't have to—"

"No. Bonnie was right, if I go to one, I should make an appearance at both. Besides, I think we're dressed fine for this one."

"Are we looking for anyone in particular, or just circulating?"

"Whichever happens first." She linked her arm through his.

Sparrow waved over the heads of assorted other people. They'd ditched their proper matron's cap and partlet for a bejeweled and befeathered turban, and an astonishing set of bling. They sashayed over, sipping from a punch cup full of fizzing neon liquid.

"How'd you beat us here?" Sophie asked.

"Darling, after the master of ceremonies informed me persons without their own partners needed to sit and wait to be asked to dance, I'd had quite enough. You know I *never* sit and wait to be asked to do *anything*. I circulated long enough to hand out business cards and chat with past customers, then I hightailed it back here."

"Is that the same dress you were wearing before?" Sam asked curiously.

"Of course it is. Accessories make all the difference."

"You look fabulous," Sophie said.

"So do you two, if I do say so myself." Someone called Sparrow's name, and they melted back into the crowd. "I'll send the things you left in my shop over to town hall tomorrow."

"Hey, Sam!" Finn appeared out of the crowd, with Bonnie beside him in all her lime-green-satin splendor. He still wore the bottom half of his costume, topped with an Otter Fest T-shirt. No one at the venue particularly cared. His arm was draped around Bonnie's shoulders and hers was wrapped around his waist.

"You look like you're having much more fun than we did."

"Told ya!" Bonnie crowed.

"I got told off for not wearing gloves. They liked the shoes, though."

"Have you checked your phone since you got back?" Finn asked.

"No." Sam fished it from his inside coat pocket. "I turned the volume off. I figured I was in enough trouble about my outfit—and apparently my haircut—without adding cell phone noises to the mix."

"You should check it. You've got a message from the director of the Regency Bay Research Center. He's offering you a position as the team's official photographer."

Sophie clutched at his arm.

"So...I'd have a job."

"How 'bout a place to stay?" Finn asked. "We could maybe squeeze in a rollaway—"

Bonnie clapped her hand over his mouth. "I think his accommodations are taken care of."

Sophie nodded.

"Besides, a roommate might cramp our style."

"La lala lalala," Sophie sang.

Bonnie stuck her tongue out.

"Did you ever have that talk? The one we

discussed?"

"Um…" Bonnie's gaze dropped to the satin rosettes on the toes of her shoes.

Finn shot Sam a puzzled glance. He shrugged.

"You know, the top of the Ferris wheel is a great place for a private conversation," Sophie hinted.

"The Ferris wheel is a great idea." Bonnie grabbed Finn's hand and dragged him off down the boardwalk.

"Let me know if I need to go shopping for itching powder!" Sophie called after them.

"Do I even want to know?" Sam asked.

"Probably not."

"Uh…she's not about to dump him two weeks before the end of the season, is she? 'Cuz if I hafta go drag him outta the Anchor at closing time because he tried to drink his weight in beer, it's really gonna put a damper on my plans for tonight."

She shook her head, grinning. "Nope. Nothing like that, I promise." She slipped her arms around his neck, and he settled his hands on her waist, his grip warm and comforting through the thin material of her gown. "Anyway, what plans do you have for the rest of the evening?"

He kissed her left cheek. "Well, I thought we'd go make your official appearance at this party." He kissed her right cheek. "Then we could—"

She grabbed the lapels of his jacket and pressed up on her toes, stealing his words with a breathless kiss. "You were saying?"

He blinked. "Or we could head back to your place and give Carb and Ginny their present." He tightened his grip on her. "And I could spend the rest of the night making up for all the trouble I've caused."

"You mean, *we* could spend the rest of the night making up for lost time."

"You're right—I like your idea much better." He kissed the end of her nose. "Soph?"

"Yes, Sam?"

"I want to be with you for the end of the summer and beginning of the Halloween murder mystery. I want to see the tiny village all decorated for Christmas and try those peppermint brownies. I want to help you plan next season. I want to do everything with you, Sophie, because I love you."

"All that, and events requiring funny clothes, and weird phone calls in the middle of the night?"

He nodded. "All of it, as long as I'm with you."

"Good, 'cuz I love you, too."

A word about the author...

I am an author with a penchant for writing about strong, sassy ladies and the men they love (and cats!). I have a background in historic and theatrical costuming. I live in New York with my cat, Miss Toby Toebeanz, who was adopted from a local rescue, in a tiny apartment with lots and lots of books.

Regency Bay is my third series with The Wild Rose Press. Destination Romance is a glamorous contemporary romance set in dazzling European locales. Carson Mills is a cozy, small-town romance about cats and the people who rescue them.